THE RAMAYANA

R. K. NARAYAN was born on October 10, 1906, in Madras, South India, and educated there and at Maharaja's College in Mysore. His first novel, *Swami and Friends* (1935), and its successor, *The Bachelor of Arts* (1937), are both set in the fictional territory of Malgudi, of which John Updike wrote, "Few writers since Dickens can match the effect of colorful teeming that Narayan's fictional city of Malgudi conveys; its population is as sharply chiseled as a temple frieze, and as endless, with always, one feels, more characters round the corner." Narayan wrote many more novels set in Malgudi, including *The English Teacher* (1945), *The Financial Expert* (1952), and *The Guide* (1958), which won him the Sahitya Akademi (India's National Academy of Letters) Award, his country's highest honor. His collections of short fiction include *A Horse and Two Goats*, *Malgudi Days*, and *Under the Banyan Tree*. Graham Greene, Narayan's friend and literary champion, said, "He has offered me a second home. Without him I could never have known what it is like to be Indian." Narayan's fiction earned him comparisons to the work of writers including Anton Chekhov, William Faulkner, O. Henry, and Flannery O'Connor.

Narayan also published travel books, volumes of essays, the memoir *My Days*, and the retold legends *Gods, Demons, and Others*, *The Ramayana*, and *The Mahabharata*. In 1980 he was awarded the A. C. Benson Medal by the Royal Society of Literature, and in 1981 he was made an Honorary Member of the American Academy of Arts and Letters. In 1989 he was made a member of the Rajya Sabha, the nonelective House of Parliament in India.

R. K. Narayan died in Madras on May 13, 2001.

PANKAJ MISHRA is the author of *The Romantics*, winner of the *Los Angeles Times*'s Art Seidenbaum Award for First Fiction, *An End to Suffering: The Buddha in the World*, and *Temptations of the West: How to be Modern in India, Pakistan, Tibet, and Beyond*. He is a frequent contributor to the *New York Times Book Review*, the *New York Review of Books*, and the *Guardian*.

R. K. NARAYAN

The Ramayana

A SHORTENED MODERN PROSE
VERSION OF THE INDIAN EPIC
(SUGGESTED BY THE TAMIL
VERSION OF KAMBAN)

Introduction by PANKAJ MISHRA

PENGUIN BOOKS

PENGUIN BOOKS

Published by the Penguin Group

Penguin Group (USA) Inc., 375 Hudson Street, New York, New York 10014, U.S.A.
Penguin Group (Canada), 90 Eglinton Avenue East, Suite 700, Toronto, Ontario,
Canada M4P 2Y3 (a division of Pearson Penguin Canada Inc.)
Penguin Books Ltd, 80 Strand, London WC2R 0RL, England
Penguin Ireland, 25 St Stephen's Green, Dublin 2, Ireland (a division of Penguin Books Ltd)
Penguin Group (Australia), 250 Camberwell Road, Camberwell, Victoria 3124,
Australia (a division of Pearson Australia Group Pty Ltd)
Penguin Books India Pvt Ltd, 11 Community Centre, Panchsheel Park,
New Delhi – 110 017, India
Penguin Group (NZ), 67 Apollo Drive, Rosedale, North Shore 0632, New Zealand
(a division of Pearson New Zealand Ltd)
Penguin Books (South Africa) (Pty) Ltd, 24 Sturdee Avenue, Rosebank,
Johannesburg 2196, South Africa

Penguin Books Ltd, Registered Offices: 80 Strand, London WC2R 0RL, England

First published in the United States of America by The Viking Press 1972
First published in Great Britain by Chatto & Windus 1973
Published in Penguin Books (U.S.A.) 1977
Published in Penguin Books (U.K) 1977
This edition with an introduction by Pankaj Mishra published in Penguin Books (U.S.A.) 2006

21 23 25 27 26 24 22 20

The decorations, drawn from Indian temple sculptures, are by R. K. Laxman.

LIBRARY OF CONGRESS CATALOGING IN PUBLICATION DATA
Narayan, R. K., 1906–2001.
The Ramayana : a shortened modern prose version of the Indian epic (suggested by the Tamil version of
Kamban) / R.K. Narayan ; introduction by Pankaj Mishra.
p. cm.—(Penguin classics)
ISBN 978-0-14-303967-9
1. Rama (Hindu deity)—Fiction.   2. Epic literature, Tamil—Adaptations.   I. Kampar, 9th cent.
Ramayanam.   II. Title.   III. Series.
PR9499.3.N3R36 2006
297.5'922—dc22   2006045201

Printed in the United States of America
Set in Sabon

Contents

Contents

Introduction

In the summer of 1988 sanitation workers across North India went on strike. Their demand was simple: they wanted the federal government to sponsor more episodes of a television serial based on the Indian epic *Ramayana* (Romance of Rama). The serial, which had been running on India's state-owned television channel for more than a year, had proved to be an extraordinarily popular phenomenon, with more than eighty million Indians tuning in to every weekly episode. Streets in all towns and cities emptied on Sunday mornings as the serial went on the air. In villages with no electricity people usually gathered around a rented television set powered by a car battery. Many bathed ritually and garlanded their television sets before settling down to watch Rama, the embodiment of righteousness, triumph over adversity.

When the government, faced with rising garbage mounds and a growing risk of epidemics, finally relented and commissioned more episodes of *The Ramayana,* not just the sanitation workers but millions of Indians celebrated. More than a decade and many reruns later, the serial continues to inspire reverence among Indians everywhere, and remains for many the primary mode of experiencing India's most popular epic.

The reasons for this may not be immediately clear to an uninitiated outsider: the serial, cheaply made by a Bollywood filmmaker, abounds in ham acting and tinselly sets, and the long, white beards of its many wise, elderly men look perilously close to dropping off.

But it wasn't so much its kitschy, Bollywood aspect that endeared the serialization to Indians as its invoking of what is easily the most influential narrative tradition in human history: the story of Rama, the unjustly exiled prince. It may be impossible to prove R. K. Narayan's claim that every Indian "is aware of the story of *The Ramayana* in some measure or other." But it will sound true to most Indians. Indeed, the popular appeal of the story of Rama among ordinary people distinguishes it from much of Indian literary tradition, which, supervised by upper-caste Hindus, has been forbiddingly elitist.

There is really no Western counterpart in either the Hellenic or Hebraic tradition to the influence that this originally secular story, transmitted orally through many centuries, has exerted over millions of people. *The Iliad* and *The Odyssey* are, primarily, literary texts, but not even Aesop's fables or the often intensely moral Greek myths shape the daily lives of present-day inhabitants of Greece. In contrast, *The Ramayana* continues to have a profound emotional and psychological resonance for Indians.

By invoking the utopian promise of Rama-Rajya (kingdom of Rama), Gandhi attracted a large mass of apolitical people to the Indian freedom movement against the British. Postcolonial India may not resemble Rama-Rajya, but the emotive appeal of *Ramayana* seems to be undiminished, and often vulnerable to political exploitation: in the late eighties and early nineties, the Hindu nationalist movement to build a temple on the alleged birthplace of Rama claimed thousands of lives across India.

* *

Like millions of other children, I first heard the story of Rama from my parents. Or so I think: I can't remember a time when I did not know it. Religious occasions at home began with a recital of the *Ramacharitamanas*, the long sixteenth-century devotional poem based on the story of Rama. All the older people I knew were only two or three decades away from village life, and they had memorized the verses in their childhood. I remember my elder sisters arguing with them about just how righteous Rama was when he killed a monkey king in cold blood or forced his wife, Sita, to undergo a test of chastity after her return from captivity.

Every autumn, I looked forward to Diwali, the most important Indian festival, which commemorates Rama's return from exile, and which children in particular love since it gives them an opportunity to buy new clothes and firecrackers and eat sweets. Autumn was also the time of the *Ramleela*, the folk pageant-play based on Rama's adventures, which is performed even today in not only all North Indian small towns and cities but also in the remote Fiji Islands and Trinidad, where descendents of nineteenth-century Indian immigrants try to hold on to their cultural links with their mother country.

I remember the performers with bare torsos, walking in an exaggerated, mincing style on their toes; Hanuman "flying" across the stage on a transparent wire; and, at the end of ten days, the burning of the big ten-headed tinsel effigy of Ravana. Armed with a bamboo bow and arrow, I imagined myself to be Rama, pursuing the forces of disorder. But it was only later I realized that though there is much of the fairytale in *The Ramayana* to engage the child—the prince thrown upon fate, the kidnapped princess, flying monkeys—it also has a complex adult and human aspect. Far from representing a straightforward battle between good and evil, it raises uncomfortable ethical and psychological questions about human motivation; it shows how greed and desire rule human beings and often make them arrogant and prone to self-deception. Even the idealized figure of Rama hints paradoxically at the difficulty of leading an ethical life.

*   *

Most versions of Rama's story begin with Dasaratha, the heirless king of Kosala who, on the urging of his spiritual advisors, performs a sacrificial ritual that enables his three wives to conceive sons. The firstborn, Rama, is the ablest and most popular of Dasaratha's offspring, who proves his superiority by stringing an enormous bow others can barely lift and by winning his bride, Sita.

When Dasaratha decides to retire from worldly duties, he chooses Rama as his successor. This greatly dismays his second wife, who wants her own son to be king. Just as the coronation of Rama is about to begin, she asks her husband to redeem two boons he had once made to her at a weak moment in his life. She demands that Rama be banished from Ayodhya for fourteen years and her son be anointed king in his place.

Dasaratha is deeply distraught by this unreasonable demand. But he is unable to refuse her—to keep one's vow is deemed one of the highest moral achievements in *The Ramayana*. Similarly, it is part of Rama's virtue to be obedient to and unquestioning of his parents. He accepts his father's decision and, accompanied by his wife, Sita, and half-brother Lakshmana, he abandons Ayodhya, much to the grief of its inhabitants.

Traveling through forests, Rama and his companions have many adventures. But none proves more dramatic than Rama's encounter one day with a demoness called Soorpanaka. She falls in love with Rama and proposes marriage to him, and then concludes that Sita's great beauty is to blame for his indifference to her. When she tries to attack Sita, Lakshmana mutilates her. Soopanaka flees to her brother Ravana, the all-powerful demon king of the island of Lanka, and tells him of the cruelty inflicted upon her.

The accounts of Sita's beauty stir Ravana's curiosity and desire. He arranges for a distraction that draws Rama and Lakshmana away from her hermitage. Then, dressed as a holy man, Ravana manages to enter Sita's dwelling and kidnaps her.

Now begins Rama's pursuit of Ravana, which leads him to unexpected friends and allies in a monkey kingdom. His most devout monkey ally, Hanuman, crosses the ocean to Lanka and alerts Sita that help is on the way. Hanuman also allows himself to be captured and produced in Ravana's court. Ravana disregards his warning of impending doom at the hands of Rama and orders Hanuman's tail to be set alight. But Hanuman escapes and, in the process, sets all of Lanka on fire. On his return, he helps Rama plan for the inevitable assault on Lanka, which comes after the monkey army builds a bridge over the ocean to the island.

After a long and bloody battle, Rama kills Ravana and his closest associates. But he suspects that Sita's virtue has not survived her long confinement in Lanka and refuses to accept her. A distraught Sita undergoes a trial by fire in order to prove her chastity, and survives. A chastened Rama returns with her to Ayodhya to be crowned king. But doubts about Sita's virtue haunt him and when he hears of rumors against her among the general public he banishes her from his kingdom. In exile she gives birth to two sons. Not long after this, she passes away, and a bereft and heartbroken Rama decides to join her in heaven.

*   *

This is the basic story on which many variations have been made through the centuries. It is not clear when it first came into being: bardic literature that has been orally transmitted cannot be precisely dated. Moreover, the story of Rama has proliferated bewilderingly across India and Southeast Asia. It exists in all major Indian languages, as well as Thai, Tibetan, Laotian, Malaysian, Chinese, Cambodian, and Javanese. In places as remote from India as Vietnam and Bali, it has been represented in countless textual and oral forms, sculpture, bas-reliefs, plays, dance-drama, and puppet plays.

Little is known about the poet Valmiki, who apparently wrote the first narrative in Sanskrit, probably around the beginning of the Christian era. Many Indians consider Valmiki's *Ramayana* to be the standard version, and it is still presented as such in many translations into English. But its version of Rama's story has been repeatedly challenged, repudiated, or simply ignored in multiple artistic forms that originate not so much from an ur-text as from what the Indian poet and critic A. K. Ramanujan called an "endemic pool of signifiers (like a gene pool)."[1]

Valmiki presented an idealized, if not beatified, image of Rama, establishing the basis for his popular reverence. Later versions present Rama as an incarnation of Lord Vishnu, the principal Hindu deity who helps preserve moral order in the world, giving epic literature a sacred dimension, and helping make *The Ramayana* part of the cult of Vishnu, one of the major cults of popular Hinduism. But many of these versions, reflecting as they do the social diversity of India, contradict one another, often self-consciously. In the version preferred by Jains, an Indian sect organized around the principles of asceticism,

Ravana is a sympathetic character, and Rama and Sita end up as world-renouncing monk and nun, respectively. The devotional *rasik* tradition in North India focuses on the marriage of Rama and Sita and ignores most of the events before and after it. The nineteenth-century Anglicized Bengali writer Michael Madhusudan Dutt chose to exalt Ravana over Rama in a long narrative poem. Ravana remains one of the heroes of low-caste Dalits in Maharashtra.

The many *Ramayana*s also reflect the ideologies of their time: like most influential literature, *The Ramayana* has never been exempt from the struggles for political power. This became clearer after the eighth century A.D. as small kingdoms arose in India, and rulers sought legitimacy through association with the cult of Rama, the supposedly ideal king (the practice continues in Thailand, where nine kings in the previous two centuries have called themselves Rama). Even during the long centuries of Muslim rule over India, people used *The Ramayana* to project the view of their particular social group. The *Ramacharitamanas,* the work of a North Indian Brahmin called Tulsi Das, laments the decay of caste hierarchy and the rise of low-caste men to positions of influence: a state of affairs that for Tulsi stands in distinctive contrast to the situation in the kingdom of Rama where everyone knew his place.

Not surprisingly, *The Ramayana* has invited its share of politically motivated critics. The South Indian activist E. V. Ramasami saw it as a tool of North Indian upper-caste domination. In an essay in 1989, the distinguished Indian historian Romila Thapar claimed that the televised *Ramayana* was an attempt to create a pan-Indian version for the more homogeneous modern age—one that India's ambitious and politically right-wing middle class could easily consume. In retrospect, Thapar seems to have been proved right: the television serial's immense popularity set the stage for the violent Hindu nationalist campaigns, in which Rama appeared as Rambo, his delicate features and gentle smile replaced by a muscular mien and grimace, and *The Ramayana* itself became a central text in the nationalists' attempt to weld Hinduism's plural traditions into a monotheistic religion.

R. K. Narayan was most certainly exposed to a benign ver-
sion of *The Ramayana* in his childhood. He would have first
imbibed it through the classical tradition of Carnatic music, the
calendar-art images and gemstone-set portraits of Rama and
Sita that are commonly found in bourgeois South Indian homes,
and the great literary classic in the Tamil language, *Kamba
Ramayana*.

But it took him some decades to get around to writing his
own version of *The Ramayana*. Born in 1906 into a rising, ur-
ban family of Tamil Brahmins, which sought to enter, with one
foot planted in tradition, the colonial Indian world of jobs and
careers, Narayan had, as a young man, a bolder ambition than
anyone around him could have possessed. He wanted to be a
"realistic fiction writer" at a time when realistic fiction writers
in English were almost entirely unknown in India. It is partly
why he was, as he relates in his memoir, *My Days* (1974), in-
different to the classical Tamil literature his uncle wanted him
to read.

Not surprisingly, Narayan wrote his abridged version of *The
Ramayana* and *The Mahabharata* only in the seventies, after
having produced some of his finest fiction: *Swami and Friends*
(1935), *The Financial Expert* (1952), *Waiting for the Mahatma*
(1955), *The Guide* (1958), and *The Vendor of Sweets* (1967).
"I was impelled," he once said, "to retell the *Ramayana* and the
Mahabharata because that was the great climate in which our
culture developed. They are symbolic and philosophical. Even
as mere stories they are so good. Marvellous. I couldn't help
writing them. It was part of the writer's discipline."[2]

The writerly compulsion Narayan expresses through his
choice of words—"impelled," "couldn't help"—seems to have
been greater than the one felt by a storyteller alighting upon
good material. There is a mythic and religious dimension to
Narayan's later fiction, in which acts of personal devotion, self-
effacement, and renunciation become a shield against the hard
demands and uncertainties of the modern, impersonal world.

This religious aspect of Narayan is explicit in his *Ramayana*.
His admiration for Rama as a cultural and social ideal is clear

throughout the book. It leads him to preface his chapter on the controversial killing of the monkey king with these rueful words.

> Rama was an ideal man, all his faculties in control in any circumstances, one possessed of an unwavering sense of justice and fair play. Yet he once acted, as it seemed, out of partiality, half-knowledge, and haste, and shot and destroyed, from hiding, a creature who had done him no harm, not even seen him.[3]

Rama's cruelty to Sita at the end of his battle with Ravana is one of the strangest episodes in *The Ramayana*—one which directly challenges Rama's image as an exemplary moral being. In fact, the Tamil poet Kamban, Narayan's literary inspiration, makes Rama say some unsettlingly harsh things to Sita.

> You stayed content in that sinner's city, enjoying your food and drink. Your good name was gone but you refused to die. How dared you think I'd be glad to have you back?[4]

But Narayan drops Kamban's account at this crucial moment in the book and chooses to bring in Valmiki's much more moderate version of Rama's decidedly odd behavior. It is as though he cannot fully acknowledge Rama's lapse into cruelty, although such an omission may also be due to Narayan's aversion to scenes of overt violence, verbal or physical—an aversion that his fiction with its careful avoidance of extremity makes clear.

Happily, Narayan doesn't linger much over battle scenes, where his prose seems to be weighed down by untranslatable archaisms. The realistic fiction writer in him is more at ease with the detail of everyday life. Here is a description of the great crowd walking to attend Rama's wedding.

> Another young man could not take his eyes off the lightly covered breast of a girl in a chariot; he tried to keep ahead of it, constantly looking back over his shoulder, unaware of what was in front, and bumping the hindquarters of the elephants on the march.[5]

Many of Narayan's virtues familiar to us from his fiction are present in this retelling of *The Ramayana*—particularly an English prose so lucid and lightly inflected that it loses its foreign associations and seems the perfect medium of swift and action-packed storytelling. Indeed, *The Ramayana* contains some of Narayan's finest prose set-pieces. Here is how he describes the end of the monsoons:

> Peacocks came out into the sun shaking off clogging droplets of water and fanning out their tails brilliantly. Rivers which had roared and overflowed now retraced their modest courses and tamely ended in the sea. Areca palms ripened their fruits in golden bunches; crocodiles emerged from the depths crawling over rocks to bask in the sun; snails vanished under slush, and crabs slipped back under ground; that rare creeper known as *vanji* suddenly burst into bloom with chattering parrots perched on its slender branches.[6]

And so instinctively scrupulous and fair-minded is Narayan as a writer that not only Rama but also Ravana emerges as a fully rounded, even somewhat sympathetic, character. Though a dedicated sensualist, Ravana does not seem intrinsically bad or evil. Narayan shows clearly how he is led astray by greed, and then succumbs to the particular illusion of power: the dream of perpetual dominance. As his younger brother, who defects to Rama's side, tells him,

> "You have acquired extraordinary powers through your own spiritual performances but you have misused your powers and attacked the very gods that gave you the power, and now you pursue evil ways. Is there anyone who has conquered the gods and lived continuously in that victory?"[7]

How often in Narayan's fiction does one come across a similar pragmatic realism, a gentle refusal to regard good and evil as unmixed, and a melancholy sense of the real limitations of life? It is this ethical and spiritual outlook that attracted countless people to *The Ramayana* for more than a millennium. In

Narayan—the sage of Malgudi who always knew how to con-
nect our hectic and fraught present to a barely remembered
past—this ancient tale found its perfect modern chronicler.

NOTES

1. A. K. Ramanujan, Paula Richman, ed., "Three Hundred Ra-
mayanas," *Many Ramayanas* (New Delhi: Oxford University
Press, 1992), 46.
2. R. K. Narayan, *The Indian Epics Retold: The Ramayana,
The Mahabharata, Gods, Demons, and Others* (New Delhi:
Penguin, 2000), xi.
3. R. K. Narayan, *The Ramayana* (New York: Penguin, 2006),
90.
4. P. S. Sundaram, trans., N. S. Jagannathan, ed., *The Kamba
Ramayana* (New Delhi: Penguin, 2002), 387.
5. Narayan, *The Ramayana*, 29.
6. Ibid., 109.
7. Ibid., 126.

Books by R. K. Narayan

NOVELS

Swami and Friends (1935)
The Bachelor of Arts (1937)
The Dark Room (1938)
The English Teacher (1945)
Mr. Sampath—The Printer of Malgudi (1949)
The Financial Expert (1952)
Waiting for the Mahatma (1955)
The Guide (1958)
The Man-Eater of Malgudi (1961)
The Vendor of Sweets (1967)
The Painter of Signs (1976)
A Tiger for Malgudi (1983)
Talkative Man (1986)
The World of Nagaraj (1990)

SHORT FICTION

*Dodu and Other Stories (1943)
*Cyclone and Other Stories (1945)
An Astrologer's Day and Other Stories (1947)
*Lawley Road and Other Stories (1956)
A Horse and Two Goats (1970)
Malgudi Days (1982)
Under the Banyan Tree and Other Stories (1985)
The Grandmother's Tale and Selected Stories (1993)

* Published in India only

RETOLD LEGENDS

Gods, Demons, and Others (1964)
The Ramayana (1972)
The Mahabharata (1978)

MEMOIR

My Days: A Memoir (1974)

NONFICTION

*Mysore (1939)
*Next Sunday: Sketches and Essays (1960)
*My Dateless Diary: An American Journey (1964)
*Reluctant Guru (1974)
*The Emerald Route (1977)
*A Writer's Nightmare: Selected Essays 1958–1988 (1988)
*A Story-Teller's World (1989)
*Indian Thought: A Miscellany (1997)
*The Writerly Life: Selected Non-fiction (2001)

* Published in India only

To the memory of my uncle
T. N. Seshachalam
who had steeped himself in
Kamban's Ramayana, and who expressed
a last wish that I should continue the study

Valmiki the poet explained to Rama himself: "Owing to the potency of your name, I became a sage, able to view the past, present, and future as one. I did not know your story yet. One day Sage Narada visited me. I asked him, 'Who is a perfect man—possessing strength, aware of obligations, truthful in an absolute way, firm in the execution of vows, compassionate, learned, attractive, self-possessed, powerful, free from anger and envy but terror-striking when roused?' Narada answered, 'Such a combination of qualities in a single person is generally rare, but one such is the very person whose name you have mastered, that is, Rama. He was born in the race of Ikshvahus, son of King Dasaratha. . . . '" And Narada narrated the story of Rama.

को न्वस्मिन्साम्प्रतं लोके गुणवान् कश्च वीर्यवान् ।
धर्मज्ञश्च कृतज्ञश्च सत्यवाक्यो दृढव्रतः ॥

चारित्रेण च को युक्तः सर्वभूतेषु को हितः ।
विद्वान्कः कस्समर्थश्च कश्चैकप्रियदर्शनः ॥

आत्मवान्को जितक्रोधः द्युतिमान्कोऽनसूयकः ।
कस्यबिभ्यति देवाश्च जातरोषस्य संयुगे ॥

एतदिच्छाम्यहं श्रोतुं परं कौतूहलं हि मे ।
महर्षे त्वं समर्थोऽसि ज्ञातुमेवंविधं नरम् ॥

बहवो दुर्लभाश्चैवयैत्वया कीर्तिताः गुणाः ।
मुने वक्ष्याम्यहं बुद्ध्वातैर्युक्तः श्रूयतां नरः ॥

Introduction

The Indian epic, the Ramayana, dates back to 1500 B.C. according to certain early scholars. Recent studies have brought it down to about the fourth century B.C. But all dates, in this regard, can only be speculative, and the later one does not diminish in any manner the intrinsic value of the great epic. It was composed by Valmiki in the classical language of India—Sanskrit. He composed the whole work, running to twenty-four thousand stanzas, in a state of pure inspiration.* It may sound hyperbolic, but I am prepared to state that almost every individual among the five hundred millions living in India is aware of the story of the Ramayana in some measure or other. Everyone of whatever age, outlook, education, or station in life knows the essential part of the epic and adores the main figures in it—Rama and Sita. Every child is told the story at bedtime. Some study it as a part of religious experience, going over a certain number of stanzas each day, reading and rereading the book several times in a lifetime. The Ramayana pervades our cultural life in one form or another at all times, it may be as a scholarly discourse at a public hall, a traditional story-teller's narrative in an open space, or a play or dance-drama on stage. Whatever the medium, the audience is always an eager one. Everyone knows the story but loves to listen to it again. One accepts this work at different levels; as a mere tale with impressive character studies; as a masterpiece of literary composition; or even as a scripture. As one's understanding develops, one discerns subtler meanings;

* The story of its composition is told in "Valmiki" in the author's *Gods, Demons, and Others.*

the symbolism becomes more defined and relevant to the day-to-day life. The Ramayana in the fullest sense of the term could be called a book of "perennial philosophy."

The Ramayana has lessons in the presentation of motives, actions and reactions, applicable for all time and for all conditions of life. Not only in areas of military, political, or economic power do we see the Ravanas—the evil antagonists—of today; but also at less conspicuous levels and in varying degrees, even in the humblest social unit or family, we can detect a Rama striving to establish peace and justice in conflict with a Ravana.

The impact of the Ramayana on a *poet*, however, goes beyond mere personal edification; it inspires him to compose the epic again in his own language, with the stamp of his own personality on it. The Ramayana has thus been the largest source of inspiration for the poets of India throughout the centuries. India is a land of many languages, each predominant in a particular area, and in each one of them a version of the Ramayana is available, original and brilliant, and appealing to millions of readers who know the language. Thus we have centuries-old Ramayana in Hindi, Bengali, Assamese, Oriya, Tamil, Kannada, Kashmiri, Telugu, Malayalam, to mention a few.

The following pages are based on a Tamil version of the epic written by a poet called Kamban of the eleventh century A.D. Tamil is a Dravidian language of great antiquity, with its own literature and cultural values, spoken by over forty millions who live in south India.*

Kamban is said to have spent every night in studying the original in Sanskrit by Valmiki, analytically, with the help of scholars, and every day in writing several thousand lines of his own poetry. Of his task in assimilating Valmiki in the original and reinterpreting him in Tamil verse, Kamban says, "I am verily like the cat sitting on the edge of an ocean of milk, hoping to lap it all up."

---

* I have given an idea of an original Tamil epic in *Gods, Demons, and Others,* in the chapter entitled "The Mispaired Anklet."

ஓசை பெற்று உயர் பாற்கடல் உற்று ஒரு
பூசை முற்றவும் நக்குப் புக்கென
ஆசை பற்றி அறையலுற்றேன் மற்றுஇக்
காசில் கொற்றத்து இராமன் கதைஅரோ.

Etched on palm leaves, Kamban's work, running to ten thousand five hundred stanzas, must have mounted into an enormous pile, as my own copy in a modern edition is in six parts, each of a thousand pages (with annotation and commentaries).

I have taken for my narration several contiguous sections of Kamban's work. Mine is by no means a translation nor a scholarly study, but may be called a resultant literary product out of the impact of Kamban on my mind as a writer. As a fiction writer, I have enjoyed reading Kamban, felt the stimulation of his poetry and the felicity of his language, admired the profundity of his thought, outlook, characterization, and sense of drama; above all the love and reverence he invokes in the reader for his main figure, Rama—who is presented to us as a youth, disciple, brother, lover, ascetic, and warrior; and in every role we watch him with awe and wonder. I have tried to convey in the following pages the delight I have experienced in Kamban.

R. K. NARAYAN
Mysore, 1971

List of Characters

(If not otherwise indicated, the "a" is broad, as in "ah"; the "th" is a soft "t" as in "thyme"; the "u" is "oo" as in "cool"; the "i" is "ee" as in "seen".)

DASARATHA (da sa ra´ ta): Emperor of the Kosala country with Ayodhya as its capital.

> KAUSALYA (kow sal´ ya)
>
> KAIKEYI (ki´ kay yee)
>
> SUMITHRA (soo mee´ tra)

wives of Dasaratha and mothers respectively of his sons RAMA, BHARATHA (ba´ rata), and the twins LAKSHMANA (lax´ ma na) and SATHRUGNA (sa troog´ na).

SUMANTHRA (soo man´ tra): Dasaratha's chief minister.

VASISHTHA (va see´ shta): royal priest to Dasaratha.

VISWAMITHRA (vee swa´ mee tra): mentor to Rama and Lakshmana; in his early years a warrior and conqueror, he transformed himself by sheer will power and austerities into an adept, teacher, and saint.* *Sage*

KOONI (koo´ nee): Kaikeyi's handmaid, whose mischief created mighty consequences.

JANAKA (ja´ na ka): King of Janaka.

SITA (see´ ta): his foster-daughter, also called JANAKI, heroine of the Ramayana (ra ma´ ya na).

SOORPANAKA (soor´ pa na ka): a demoness, sister to RAVANA (below), KARA: commander of her army of demons.

*See "Viswamitra" in *Gods, Demons, and Others.*

JATAYU (ja ta´ yoo): a great eagle pledged to guard the lives of Dasaratha's children.

SAMPATHI (sam´ pa ti): Jatayu's elder brother, deformed for challenging the sun, restored on hearing Rama's name.

VALI (va´ lee): ruler of Kiskinda, peopled by a giant monkey race.

SUGREEVA (soo gree´ va): his brother, who engineers his death with Rama's help.

TARA: Vali's wife.

ANGADA (an´ ga da): Vali's son.

HANUMAN (ha´ noo man): Sugreeva's ally, also called ANJANEYA (an´ ja nay ya), the greatest devotee of Rama; son of the god of wind, possessing immeasurable strength, energy, and wisdom.

JAMBAVAN (jam ba´ van): one of the wise elders of Hanuman's search party, now in the form of a bear.

THATAKA (ta´ ta ka): a demoness, daughter of SUKETHA (soo keé ta) and wife of SUNDA (soon´da).

SUBAHU (soo ba´ hoo) and MAREECHA (ma ree´ cha): her sons.

RAVANA (ra´ va na): ruler of Lanka.

VIBISHANA (vee bee´ sha na)
KUMBAKARNA (koom´ ba kar´ na) } his brothers.

INDRAJIT (een dra´ jeet): his son.

MANDODARI (man dō´ da ree): his wife.

In the Tales:

GAUTAMA (gow´ ta ma): a sage who cursed his wife, AHALYA (a hal´ ya), turned to stone for infidelity.

BHAGIRATHA (ba ghee´ ra ta): who by his stubborn effort brought the Ganges down to earth in order to obtain salvation for his ancestors by washing their bones in its waters.

MAHABALI (ma ha´ ba lee): a demoniac conqueror of several worlds; to end his tyranny Vishnu incarnated as a pigmy called VAMANA (va´ ma na).

MAHAVISHNU (ma ha´ vish noo): the Supreme God, who divides himself into a trinity named Brahma, Vishnu, and Shiva for the actual functioning of the universe with all its beings.

The Ramayana

Prologue

In keeping with the classical tradition, Kamban begins his epic with a description of the land in which the story is set. The first stanza mentions the river Sarayu, which flows through the country of Kosala. The second stanza lifts your vision skyward to observe the white fleecy clouds that drift across the sky towards the sea, and later return in dark water-laden masses to the mountaintops, where they condense and flow down the slopes in streams scouring the mountainside of its treasures of minerals and essences ("verily like a woman of pleasure gently detaching the valuables from her patron during her caresses"). The river descends with a load of merchandise such as precious stones, sandalwood, peacock feathers, and iridescent flower petals and pollen grains, carrying it through the mountains, forests, valleys, and plains of Kosala country, and, after evenly distributing the gifts, ends its career in the sea.

The poet then describes the countryside with its gardens and groves; its men and women fully occupied, their activities ranging from tilling, harvesting, and threshing to watching cockfights of an afternoon. In the background, the perpetual groan of mills crushing sugarcane or corn, bellowing of cattle, or clamour of bullock-drawn caravans loaded with produce departing for far-off lands. Different kinds of smoke rise in the air, from kitchen chimneys, kilns, sacrificial fires, and fragrant wood burnt for incense. Different kinds of nectar—juices of sugarcane and palmyra, the dew in the heart of a chrysanthemum or lotus, or the well-stocked hive under aromatic trees—these fed the honey-bees as well as tiny birds that survived only on such nourishment; even the fishes relished this sweetness dripping and flowing into the river. At one temple or another, a festival or a wedding is always being celebrated with drums and pipes and procession. Kamban describes every sound, sight, and smell of the country, even to the extent of mentioning garbage heaps with crows and hens busily scratching and searching them.

Kosala was an extensive country and few could claim to have crossed it end to end. Ayodhya was its capital—a city of palaces, mansions, fountains, squares, and ramparts with the King's palace dominating the landscape. The city was imposing and compared well with the fabulous city of Amravati which was Indra's or Alkapuri of Kubera. Presiding over this capital and the country was King Dasaratha, who ruled with compassion and courage and was loved and honoured by his subjects, and was blessed in many ways. His one great sorrow in life was that he was childless.

One day he summoned his mentor at the court, Sage Vasishtha, and said to him, "I am in a sad plight. The solar dynasty is likely to end with me. I shall have no successor when I am no more. This thought torments me. Please tell me how can I remedy it."

At this Vasishtha recollected an incident that he had witnessed through his inner vision. At one time all the gods went in a body to appeal to the Supreme God Vishnu for his help. They explained, "The ten-headed Ravana and his brothers have acquired from us extraordinary powers through austerities and prayers, and now threaten to destroy our worlds and enslave us. They go along recklessly in their career of tyranny, suppressing all virtue and goodness wherever found. Shiva is unable to help; Brahma the Creator can do very little, since the powers that Ravana and his brothers are now misusing were originally conferred by these two gods, and cannot be withdrawn by them. You alone are the Protector and should save us." Whereupon Vishnu promised, "Ravana can be destroyed only by a human being since he never asked for protection from a human being. I shall incarnate as Dasaratha's son, and my conch and my wheel, which I hold in each hand for certain purposes, and my couch, namely Adisesha, the Serpent, on whose coils I rest, shall be born as my brothers, and all the gods here shall take birth in the world below in a monkey clan—since Ravana has been cursed in earlier times to expect his destruction only from a monkey."

Recollecting this episode, but without mentioning it, Vasishtha advised Dasaratha, "You must immediately arrange for the performance of a *yagna*. The only person who is competent to conduct such a sacrifice is Sage Rishya Sringa."

Dasaratha asked, "Where is he? How can I bring him here?"

Vasishtha answered, "At the present time, Rishya Sringa is in our neighbouring country, Anga."

Dasaratha exclaimed, "Oh, how fortunate! I thought he was far off in his mountain fastness."

And then Vasishtha explained, "In order to end a prolonged drought, the King of Anga was advised to get Rishya Sringa to visit his country, since it always rained in his proximity; but they knew that on no account would he consent to leave his mountain retreat. While the King was considering how to solve the problem, a bevy of beauties offered their services and went forth in search of this young sage. They reached his hermitage, found him alone, and enticed him away to Anga. He had never seen any human being except his father, and could not make out what these creatures were, when the damsels from Anga surrounded him. But given time for instinct to work, he became curious and abandoned himself to their care. They represented themselves as ascetics, invited him to visit their hermitage, and carried him away." (In Mysore State at Kigga, four thousand feet above sea level, a carving on a temple pillar shows the young recluse being carried off on a palanquin made of the intertwined arms of naked women.) "On his arrival at Anga, the rains came. The King was pleased, rewarded the ladies, and persuaded the young man to marry his daughter and settle down at his court."

Dasaratha journeyed to Anga and invited the sage to visit Ayodhya. A sacrifice was held under his guidance; it went on for one full year, at the end of which an immense supernatural being emerged from the sacrificial fire bearing in his arms a silver plate with a bolus of sacramental rice on it. He placed it beside King Dasaratha and vanished back into the fire.

Rishya Sringa advised the King, "Take the rice and divide it among your wives and they will have children." In proper time, Dasaratha's wives, Kausalya and Kaikeyi, gave birth to Rama and Bharatha respectively, and Sumithra gave birth to Lakshmana and Sathrugna.

Dasaratha's life attained a fuller meaning, and he felt extremely happy as he watched his children grow. At each stage, he engaged tutors for their training and development. In course of time, every morning, the young men went to the groves on the outskirts and learned yoga and philosophy from the adepts residing there. Late in the evening, after the lessons, when the princes returned to the palace on foot, the citizens crowded the highway to have a glimpse of them. Rama always had a word for everyone in the crowd, inquiring, "How are you? Are your children happy? Do you want any help from me?" They always answered, "With you as our prince and your great father as our guardian, we lack nothing."

I
RAMA'S INITIATION

The new assembly hall, Dasaratha's latest pride, was crowded all day with visiting dignitaries, royal emissaries, and citizens coming in with representations or appeals for justice. The King was always accessible, and fulfilled his duties as the ruler of Kosala without grudging the hours spent in public service.

On a certain afternoon, messengers at the gate came running in to announce, "Sage Viswamithra." When the message was relayed to the King, he got up and hurried forward to receive the visitor. Viswamithra, once a king, a conqueror, and a dreaded name until he renounced his kingly role and chose to become a sage (which he accomplished through severe austerities), combined in himself the sage's eminence and the king's authority and was quick tempered and positive. Dasaratha led him to a proper seat and said, "This is a day of glory for us; your gracious presence is most welcome. You must have come from afar. Would you first rest?"

"No need," the sage replied simply. He had complete mastery over his bodily needs through inner discipline and austerities, and was above the effects of heat, cold, hunger, fatigue, and even decrepitude. The King later asked politely, "Is there anything I can do?" Viswamithra looked steadily at the King and answered, "Yes. I am here to ask of you a favour. I wish to perform, before the next full moon, a yagna at Sidhasrama. Doubtless you know where it is?"

"I have passed that sacred ground beyond the Ganges many times."

The sage interrupted. "But there are creatures hovering about waiting to disturb every holy undertaking there, who must be overcome in the same manner as one has to conquer the five-fold evils* within before one can realize holiness. Those evil creatures are endowed with immeasurable powers of destruction. But it is our duty to pursue our aims undeterred. The yagna I propose to perform will strengthen the beneficial forces of this world, and please the gods above."

"It is my duty to protect your sublime effort. Tell me when, and I will be there."

The sage said, "No need to disturb your august self. Send your son Rama with me, and he will help me. He can."

"Rama!" cried the King, surprised, "When I am here to serve you."

Viswamithra's temper was already stirring. "I know your greatness," he said, cutting the King short. "But I want Rama to go with me. If you are not willing, you may say so."

The air became suddenly tense. The assembly, the ministers and officials, watched in solemn silence. The King looked miserable. "Rama is still a child, still learning the arts and practising the use of arms." His sentences never seemed to conclude, but trailed away as he tried to explain. "He is a boy, a child, he is too young and tender to contend with demons."

"But I know Rama," was all that Viswamithra said in reply.

"I can send you an army, or myself lead an army to guard your performance. What can a stripling like Rama do against those terrible forces . . . ? I will help you just as I helped Indra once when he was harassed and deprived of his kingdom."

Viswamithra ignored his speech and rose to leave. "If you cannot send Rama, I need none else." He started to move down the passage.

The King was too stricken to move. When Viswamithra had gone half way, he realized that the visitor was leaving unceremoniously and was not even shown the courtesy of being escorted to the door. Vasishtha, the King's priest and guide, whispered to Dasaratha, "Follow him and call him back," and hurried forward even before the King could grasp what he was saying. He almost ran as Viswamithra had reached the end of

*Lust, anger, miserliness, egoism, envy.

the hall and, blocking his way, said, "The King is coming; please don't go. He did not mean . . ."

A wry smile played on Viswamithra's face as he said without any trace of bitterness, "Why are you or anyone agitated? I came here for a purpose; it has failed; no reason to prolong my stay."

"Oh, eminent one, you were yourself a king once."

"What has that to do with us now?" asked Viswamithra, rather irked, since he hated all reference to his secular past and wanted always to be known as a Brahma Rishi.

Vasishtha answered mildly, "Only to remind you of an ordinary man's feelings, especially a man like Dasaratha who had been childless and had to pray hard for an issue. . . ."

"Well, it may be so, great one; I still say that I came on a mission and wish to leave, since it has failed."

"It has not failed," said Vasishtha, and just then the King came up to join them in the passage; the assembly was on its feet.

Dasaratha made a deep obeisance and said, "Come back to your seat, Your Holiness."

"For what purpose, Your Majesty?" Viswamithra asked.

"Easier to talk seated . . ."

"I don't believe in any talk," said Viswamithra; but Vasishtha pleaded with him until he returned to his seat.

When they were all seated again, Vasishtha addressed the King: "There must be a divine purpose working through this seer, who may know but will not explain. It is a privilege that Rama's help should be sought. Do not bar his way. Let him go with the sage."

"When, oh when?" the King asked anxiously.

"Now," said Viswamithra. The King looked woebegone and desperate, and the sage relented enough to utter a word of comfort. "You cannot count on the physical proximity of someone you love, all the time. A seed that sprouts at the foot of its parent tree remains stunted until it is transplanted. Rama will be in my care, and he will be quite well. But ultimately, he will leave me too. Every human being, when the time comes, has to depart and seek his fulfillment in his own way."

"Sidhasrama is far away . . . ?" began the King.

"I'll ease his path for him, no need for a chariot to take us there," said Viswamithra reading his mind.

"Rama has never been separated from his brother Laksh-mana. May he also go with him?" pleaded the King, and he looked relieved when he heard Viswamithra say, "Yes, I will look after both, though their mission will be to look after me. Let them get ready to follow me; let them select their favourite weapons and prepare to leave."

Dasaratha, with the look of one delivering hostages into the hand of an enemy, turned to his minister and said, "Fetch my sons."

Following the footsteps of their master like his shadows, Rama and Lakshmana went past the limits of the city and reached the Sarayu River, which bounded the capital on the north. When night fell, they rested at a wooded grove and at dawn crossed the river. When the sun came over the mountain peak, they reached a pleasant grove over which hung, like a canopy, fragrant smoke from numerous sacrificial fires. Viswamithra explained to Rama, "This is where God Shiva meditated once upon a time and re-duced to ashes the god of love when he attempted to spoil his meditation.* From time immemorial saints praying to Shiva come here to perform their sacrifices, and the pall of smoke you notice is from their sacrificial fires."

A group of hermits emerged from their seclusion, received Viswamithra, and invited him and his two disciples to stay with them for the night. Viswamithra resumed his journey at dawn and reached a desert region at midday. The mere expression "desert" hardly conveys the absolute aridity of this land. Under a relentless sun, all vegetation had dried and turned to dust, stone and rock crumbled into powdery sand, which lay in vast dunes, stretching away to the horizon. Here every inch was scorched and dry and hot beyond imagination. The ground was cracked and split, exposing enormous fissures everywhere. The distinction be-tween dawn, noon, and evening did not exist here, as the sun seemed to stay overhead and burn the earth without moving. Bleached bones lay where animals had perished, including those of monstrous serpents with jaws open in deadly thirst; into these

*See "Manmata" in *Gods, Demons, and Others.*

enormous jaws had rushed (says the poet) elephants desperately seeking shade, all dead and fossilized, the serpent and the elephant alike. Heat haze rose and singed the very heavens. While traversing this ground, Viswamithra noticed the bewilderment and distress on the faces of the young men, and transmitted to them mentally two *mantras* (called "Bala" and "Adi-Bala"). When they meditated on and recited these incantations, the arid atmosphere was transformed for the rest of their passage and they felt as if they were wading through a cool stream with a southern summer breeze blowing in their faces. Rama, ever curious to know the country he was passing through, asked, "Why is this land so terrible? Why does it seem accursed?"

"You will learn the answer if you listen to this story—of a woman fierce, ruthless, eating and digesting all living creatures, possessing the strength of a thousand mad elephants."

THATAKA'S STORY

The woman I speak of was the daughter of Suketha, a *yaksha*, a demigod of great valour, might, and purity. She was beautiful and full of wild energy. When she grew up she was married to a chieftain named Sunda. Two sons were born to them—Mareecha and Subahu—who were endowed with enormous supernatural powers in addition to physical strength; and in their conceit and exuberance they laid waste their surroundings. Their father, delighted at their pranks and infected by their mood, joined in their activities. He pulled out ancient trees by their roots and flung them about, and he slaughtered all creatures that came his way. This depredation came to the notice of the great savant Agasthya (the diminutive saint who once, when certain demoniac beings hid themselves at the bottom of the sea and Indra appealed for his help to track them, had sipped off the waters of the ocean). Agasthya had his hermitage in this forest, and when he noticed the destruction around, he cursed the perpetrator of this deed and Sunda fell dead. When his wife learnt of his death, she and her sons stormed in, roaring revenge on the saint. He met their challenge by cursing them. "Since you are destroyers of

life, may you become *asuras* and dwell in the nether worlds."
(Till now they had been demigods. Now they were degraded to
demonhood.) The three at once underwent a transformation;
their features and stature became forbidding, and their natures
changed to match. The sons left to seek the company of su-
perdemons. The mother was left alone and lives on here,
breathing fire and wishing everything ill. Nothing flourishes
here; only heat and sand remain. She is a scorcher. She carries
a trident with spikes; a cobra entwined on her arm is her arm-
let. The name of this fearsome creature is Thataka. Just as the
presence of a little *loba* (meanness) dries up and disfigures a
whole human personality, so does the presence of this monster
turn into desert a region which was once fertile. In her rest-
lessness she constantly harasses the hermits at their prayers;
she gobbles up anything that moves and sends it down her en-
trails.

*   *

Touching the bow slung on his shoulder, Rama asked,
"Where is she to be found?"

Before Viswamithra could answer, she arrived, the ground
rocking under her feet and a storm preceding her. She loomed
over them with her eyes spitting fire, her fangs bared, her lips
parted revealing a cavernous mouth; and her brows twitching in
rage. She raised her trident and roared, "In this my kingdom, I
have crushed out the minutest womb of life and you have been
sent down so that I may not remain hungry."

Rama hesitated; for all her evil, she was still a woman. How
could he kill her? Reading his thoughts, Viswamithra said,
"You shall not consider her a woman at all. Such a monster
must receive no consideration. Her strength, ruthlessness, ap-
pearance, rule her out of that category. Formerly God Vishnu
himself killed Kyathi, the wife of Brigu, who harboured the
asuras fleeing his wrath, when she refused to yield them. Man-
dorai, a woman bent upon destroying all the worlds, was van-
quished by Indra and he earned the gratitude of humanity.
These are but two instances. A woman of demoniac tendencies
loses all consideration to be treated as a woman. This Thataka

is more dreadful than Yama, the god of death, who takes a life only when the time is ripe. But this monster, at the very scent of a living creature, craves to kill and eat. Do not picture her as a woman at all. You must rid this world of her. It is your duty."

Rama said, "I will carry out your wish."

Thataka threw her three-pronged spear at Rama. As it came flaming, Rama strung his bow and sent an arrow which broke it into fragments. Next she raised a hail of stones under which to crush her adversaries. Rama sent up his arrows, which shielded them from the attack. Finally Rama's arrow pierced her throat and ended her career; thereby also inaugurating Rama's life's mission of destroying evil and demonry in this world. The gods assembled in the sky and expressed their joy and relief and enjoined Viswamithra, "Oh, adept and master of weapons, impart without any reserve all your knowledge and powers to this lad. He is a saviour." Viswamithra obeyed this injunction and taught Rama all the esoteric techniques in weaponry. Thereafter the presiding deities of various weapons, *asthras,* appeared before Rama submissively and declared, "Now we are yours; command us night or day."

When they reached a mist-covered wood on a mountain, Viswamithra told another story.

MAHABALI'S STORY

This is consecrated ground where Vishnu once sat in meditation. (Although Rama was Vishnu, his human incarnation made him unaware of his identity at the moment.) While Vishnu was thus engaged, Mahabali seized the earth and heaven and brought them under his subjection. He celebrated his victory by performing a great yagna, and used this occasion to invite and honour all learned men. All the gods who had suffered in their encounter with Mahabali arrived in a body at the spot where Vishnu was in meditation and begged him to help them regain their kingdoms. In response to their appeals, Vishnu took birth in a brahmin family as a person of tiny proportions; within this diminutive personality was packed a great deal of power and learning. Mahabali was quick to sense his greatness when this dwarfish man presented himself at the palace gate. Mahabali received the visitor warmly and respectfully.

The visitor said, "I have come from afar after hearing of your greatness. My ambition in life has been to have a glimpse of one who is renowned alike for his valour and generosity. Now, after meeting you, I have attained my life's ambition. Achievements such as yours cannot be measured. When a poor man like me has a glimpse of your divinity, a part of it comes to me also."

"Oh great one, do not praise me," Mahabali replied. "I am after all a fighter and conqueror—base qualities when compared to the learning and special attainments of one like you. I am not easily led by appearances. I can know how great you must be. I shall be happy if you will accept a gift in return for the honour you have done in visiting me."

"I want nothing. I need no gift other than your goodwill."

"No, please don't go, ask for something, mention anything you want. It will please me to grant it."

"If you insist, then give me a piece of land."

"Yes, choose it wherever you like."

"Not more than what would be measured in three strides of my feet . . ."

Bali laughed, looked him up and down, and said, "Is that all?"

"Yes."

"I shall now . . . ," began Mahabali, but before he could complete his sentence, his guru Sukracharya interrupted to warn, "King, do not be rash. The small figure you see is a deception: he is minute, but this microcosm . . ."

"Oh, stop! I know my responsibility. To give while one can is the right time, and to prevent a gift is an unholy act, unworthy of you. He who is selfish is never worse than the one who stays the hand that is about to give. Don't stop me," he said; and poured out a little water from a vessel on the upturned palm of the little man to seal his promise. (It is found in some texts that at this moment Sukracharya assumed the size of a bee and flew into the spout of the vessel in order to block the flow of water and thus prevent the oath being given. The dwarf, sensing this, took a sharp *dharba* grass and thrust it in to clear the obstruction and it pricked the eye of Sukracharya, who thereafter came to be known as the one-eyed savant.) Pouring this oblation of water, Bali said to the little man, "Now measure and take your three steps of earth."

The moment the water fell on his hand, this person, who was a figure of fun even to his parents till then, assumed a majestic stature spanning the earth and the sky. With the first step he measured the entire earth, with the second he covered the heavens. No more space was left in the whole universe, and he asked Mahabali, "Where shall I place the third step?"

Mahabali, overawed, knelt, bowed, and said, "Here on my head, if no other space is available." Vishnu raised his foot, placed it on Mahabali's head, and pressed him down to the netherworld. "You may stay there," he said, and thus disposed of the tormentor of the worlds.

*   *

Concluding the story, Viswamithra announced, "This is the end of our journey for the time being. Here I will perform the sacrifices under your protection."

In due course Viswamithra gathered a good company of saints and made preparations for the yagna, Rama and Lakshmana guarding the ground. Meanwhile the asuras assembled in the skies above the holy ground, ready to disrupt the yagna. The demons were armed with a variety of deadly weapons; they shrieked and howled and attempted in other ways to create confusion. They flung boiling water and offal on the holy ground; uttered menaces, curses, and blasphemies; tore out huge rocks and flung them down; and set in force terrifying magical disturbances.

The saints looked distraught. Rama advised the sages, "Do not feel disturbed. Proceed with your prayers."

Lakshmana said to Rama, "I will deal with them." He shot at them, while Rama sent up his arrows and created an umbrella to shield the sacrificial fire from being defiled by the asuras' blood. Subahu and Mareecha, the sons of Thataka thought this their best chance to avenge the death of their mother and aimed their attack at Rama, whose first shot carried Mareecha far out and threw him into the sea; the second one eliminated Subahu. The demons who had gathered with such zest withdrew in panic.

The sacrifice was successfully accomplished. Viswamithra declared, "Rama, you alone could help me in this task. This was performed not for my personal satisfaction, but for the good of humanity itself."

Rama asked, "What next?"

Viswamithra said, "You have accomplished much now. There is a great deal yet ahead of you," hinting at the tasks that Rama would have to fulfill in this incarnation. "For the present let us proceed towards Mithila City, where a great yagna is to be performed by King Janaka, and where many others will be arriving; you may enjoy this diversion." Although he suggested this step as a sort of relaxation for Rama, he knew by foresight that it was but the beginning of a great series of events in which Rama's future would be involved.

At the end of a day's journeying, they arrived at a valley where the Ganges was flowing. "There you see," said Viswamithra, "the river Ganga, the holiest river in the world, starting from the Himalayas, running her course through mountains and valleys and across several kingdoms. Today she flows along peacefully, but at the beginning . . . Now listen to her story."

GANGA'S STORY

Every inch of ground on earth, as you may have realized by now, has a divine association. Mother Earth has been there since the beginning of creation, being one of the five primeval elements. She has seen countless pairs of feet running about on thousands of aims and pursuits, both evil and good, and will continue until Time ("Kala") swallows and digests everything. Even after the participants have vanished, every inch of earth still retains the impress of all that has gone before. We attain a full understanding only when we are aware of the divine and other associations of every piece of ground we tread on. Otherwise it would be like the passage of a blind man through illuminated halls and gardens. That is the reason why I have explained to you the story of every place we have passed through. You see that river now. It is Ganga flowing along the valley, coming down from the Himalayas, carrying within her the essence of rare herbs and elements found on her way. She courses through many a kingdom, and every inch of the ground she touches becomes holy; Ganga cleanses and transforms; the dying person with a sip of that water or with the ashes of his bones dissolved therein attains salvation. Now you find the river serene and beautiful. But Ganga had to be tamed and controlled before she could touch this earth; her story involves the fate of your ancestors, very early ones.

Sakara, one of your ancestors, ruled the earth with great distinction at one time. He had numerous sons, all valorous and devoted to their father. At the proper time in his career, he planned to perform a very important sacrifice—the "Horse Sacrifice."

In preparation for this ceremony a resplendent horse fully caparisoned and decorated is set free and trots along at will through the frontiers of many kingdoms, and every country that lets the horse pass through is considered to have accepted the suzerainty of the horse's owner. But if at any point anyone attempts to hold up the horse, it is taken as a challenge and causes a war; the original owner of the horse attacks the country where the horse is held and sets it free again, and again and again until it gets through and returns home. Then all the countries through which it has passed become vassals of the king, and the king celebrates his victory with the great "Horse Sacrifice" which makes him supreme lord of the earth. Those who embark on such a plan are confident of victory and could eventually aspire to extend their empire and challenge Indra himself. Hence Indra and all the gods are very watchful and nervous whenever a sacrifice is planned, and do their best to defeat it.

When Sakara's horse started out Indra abducted it and kept it out of view in the deepest world underground, behind Sage Kapila, who had earlier sought this seclusion far away from the earth for his spiritual practices. When it became known that the horse was lost underground, Sakara's sons started digging wide and deep and went down into the bowels of the earth. They found their horse tethered behind the man in meditation; they seized the horse and tormented the saint, assuming that he had stolen it; whereupon the saint with an angry glare reduced them to ashes. One of the party survived this expedition, a grandson of the emperor; he apologized to the sage and came home and helped the old king to complete his "Horse Sacrifice." Later, King Sakara renounced the world in favour of his grandson, whose son was Bhagiratha, responsible for bringing the Ganges down to earth.

When Bhagiratha grew up and learnt of the fate of his ancestors, he made it his mission in life to help them attain salvation, instead of leaving their spirits dangling in mid-air without proper disposal of their remains. He prayed intensely for ten thousand years to Brahma, the creator, who advised him to seek the help of Shiva to bring down Ganga from high heaven and to wash their bones in the holy water. He prayed to Shiva for ten thousand years and he appeared and promised to grant his wishes if he could somehow persuade Ganga to descend. And then he prayed to Ganga for five thousand years. Ganga appeared to him in the guise of an elegant little girl and said, "Shiva has promised you his help, no doubt, but if Ganga descends in her full force, the earth will not bear it; nothing can ever bear the force of her descent. Shiva agreed to help you—but find out what his intentions are. Pray to him again."

After further meditations, by Bhagiratha, Shiva again appeared and said to him, "Let Ganga come down, I will help you. I will see that no drop of that water is wasted or allowed to trouble anyone." This was developing into a series of challenges between Shiva and Ganga, and Bhagiratha began to feel that he was being tossed between challenging gods. But undaunted (his name is a byword for indefatigable effort), he had prayed for thirty thousand years in all, undergoing severe austerities—such as living on dry fallen leaves, then on air, then on sun's rays, and in the last stages he gave up even these and survived on practically nothing, conscious of nothing but his own purpose and faith in his cause.

At the end of Bhagiratha's penance, Ganga, whose origin was in the far-off world of Brahma, the creator, started her descent in a roaring deluge. As promised, Shiva appeared on the scene just when the deluge was about to hit and pulverize the earth.

Shiva took his stance, planted his feet firmly, arms akimbo, and received the impact of the descent on his head, and the threatened deluge just vanished into his tangled, matted locks. For all the uproar and conceit that Ganga had displayed this was a tame end—so tame and quiet indeed that Bhagiratha began to feel uneasy. It seemed as if this was the end of Ganga and that all his prayers and penances had produced nothing in the end. Shiva understood his fears and let a trickle out of his hair which Bhagiratha led on carefully and anxiously underground over his ancestors' ashes and helped their souls attain salvation. Thus Bhagiratha helped not only his ancestors, but all mankind, as the Ganges bears a countless number of holy shrines on its banks, and nourishes millions of acres of land and people along its course. The pit dug by Sakara's sons while searching for their horse also filled up and became the oceans of today.

* *

They arrived within sight of Mithila City. While passing over slightly raised ground beside the walls of the fort, Rama noticed a shapeless slab of stone, half buried vertically in the ground; when he brushed past, the dust of his feet fell on it, and transformed it, that very instant, into a beautiful woman. As the woman did obeisance and stood aside respectfully, Viswamithra introduced her to Rama. "If you have heard of Sage Gautama, whose curse resulted in great Indra's body being studded with a thousand eyes, all over . . . This lady was his wife, and her name is Ahalya." And he told Rama her story.

AHALYA'S STORY

Brahma once created, out of the ingredients of absolute beauty, a woman, and she was called Ahalya (which in the Sanskrit language means non-imperfection). God Indra, being the highest god among the gods, was attracted by her beauty and was convinced that he alone was worthy of claiming her hand. Brahma, noticing the conceit and presumptuousness of Indra, ignored him, sought out Sage Gautama, and left him in charge of the

girl. She grew up in his custody, and when the time came the
sage took her back to Brahma and handed her over to him.

Brahma appreciated Gautama's purity of mind and heart
(never once had any carnal thought crossed his mind), and said,
"Marry her, she is fit to be your wife, or rather you alone de-
serve to be her husband." Accordingly, she was married, blessed
by Brahma and other gods. Having spent her childhood with
Gautama, Ahalya knew his needs and so proved a perfect wife,
and they lived happily.

Indra, however, never got over his infatuation for Ahalya, and
often came in different guises near to Gautama's *ashram*, waiting
for every chance to gaze and feast on Ahalya's form and figure;
he also watched the habits of the sage and noticed that the sage
left his ashram at the dawn of each day and was away for a cou-
ple of hours at the river for his bath and prayers. Unable to bear
the pangs of love any more, Indra decided to attain the woman of
his heart by subterfuge. One day, hardly able to wait for the sage
to leave at his usual hour, Indra assumed the voice of a rooster,
and woke up the sage, who, thinking that the morning had come,
left for the river. Now Indra assumed the sage's form, entered the
hut, and made love to Ahalya. She surrendered herself, but at
some stage realized that the man enjoying her was an imposter;
but she could do nothing about it. Gautama came back at this
moment, having intuitively felt that something was wrong, and
surprised the couple in bed. Ahalya stood aside filled with shame
and remorse; Indra assumed the form of a cat (the most facile an-
imal form for sneaking in or out) and tried to slip away. The sage
looked from the cat to the woman and was not to be deceived.
He arrested the cat where he was with these words:

"Cat, I know you; your obsession with the female is your
undoing. May your body be covered with a thousand female
marks, so that in all the worlds, people may understand what
really goes on in your mind all the time." Hardly had these
words left his lips when every inch of Indra's body displayed the
female organ. There could be no greater shame for the proud
and self-preening Indra.

After Indra slunk away, back to his world, Gautama looked at
his wife and said, "You have sinned with your body. May that

body harden into a shapeless piece of granite, just where you are. . . ." Now in desperation Ahalya implored, "A grave mistake has been committed. It is in the nature of noble souls to forgive the errors of lesser beings. Please . . . I am already feeling a weight creeping up my feet. Do something . . . please help me. . . ."

Now the sage felt sorry for her and said, "Your redemption will come when the son of Dasaratha, Rama, passes this way at some future date. . . ."

"When? Where?" she essayed to question, desperately, but before the words could leave her lips she had become a piece of stone.

Indra's predicament became a joke in all the worlds at first, but later proved noticeably tragic. He stayed in darkness and seclusion and could never appear before men or women. This caused much concern to all the gods, as his multifarious duties in various worlds remained suspended, and they went in a body to Brahma and requested him to intercede with Gautama. By this time, the sage's resentment had vanished. And he said in response to Brahma's appeal, "May the thousand additions to Indra's features become eyes." Indra thereafter came to be known as the "thousand-eyed god."

* *

Viswamithra concluded the story and addressed Rama. "O great one, you are born to restore righteousness and virtue to mankind and eliminate all evil. At our yagna, I saw the power of your arms, and now I see the greatness of the touch of your feet."

Rama said to Ahalya, "May you seek and join your revered husband, and live in his service again. Let not your heart be burdened with what is past and gone."

On their way to Mithila, they stopped to rest at Gautama's hermitage, and Viswamithra told the sage, "Your wife is restored to her normal form, by the touch of Rama's feet. Go and take her back, her heart is purified through the ordeal she has undergone." All this accomplished, they moved on, leaving behind the scented groves and forest, and approached the battlemented gates of Mithila City.

2
THE WEDDING

Mithila, after all the forests, mountain paths, valleys, and places of solitude and silence through which we have travelled thus far, offers a pleasant change to a city of colour and pleasure, with people enjoying the business of living. The very minute Rama steps into Mithila, he notices golden turrets and domes, and towers, and colourful flags fluttering in the wind as if to welcome a royal bridegroom-to-be. The streets glitter with odds and ends of jewellery cast off by the people (a necklace that had snapped during a dance or a game; or had been flung off when found to be a nuisance during an embrace), with no one inclined to pick them up in a society of such affluence. There was no charity in Kosala country since there was no one to receive it. Torn-off flower garlands lay in heaps on the roadside with honey-bees swarming over them. The *musth* running down the haunches of mountainous elephants flowed in dark streams along the main thoroughfare, blending with the white froth dripping from the mouths of galloping horses, and churned with mud and dust by ever-turning chariot wheels.

On lofty terraces women were singing and dancing to the accompaniment of *veena* and soft drums. Couples on swings suspended from tall *areca* poles enjoyed the delight of swaying back and forth, their necklaces or garlands flying in the air. Rama and Lakshmana went on past shops displaying gems, gold, ivory, peacock feathers, beads, and wigs made of the hair of rare Himalayan deer. They observed arenas where strange elephant fights were in progress, cheered by crowds of young men; groups of women practising ballads and love songs under wayside

canopies; horses galloping without a break round and round
bridle tracks, watched by elegant men and women; swimming
pools with multicoloured fish agitated by people sporting in the
water.

They crossed the moat surrounding Janaka's palace, with its
golden spires soaring above the other buildings of the city. Now
Rama observed on a balcony princess Sita playing with her
companions. He stood arrested by her beauty, and she noticed
him at the same moment. Their eyes met. They had been together
not so long ago in Vaikunta, their original home in heaven, as
Vishnu and his spouse Lakshmi, but in their present incarna-
tion, suffering all the limitations of mortals, they looked at
each other as strangers. Sita, decked in ornaments and flowers,
in the midst of her attendants, flashed on his eyes like a streak
of lightning. She paused to watch Rama slowly pass out of
view, along with his sage-master and brother. The moment he
vanished, her mind became uncontrollably agitated. The eye
had admitted a slender shaft of love, which later expanded and
spread into her whole being. She felt ill.

Observing the sudden change in her, and the sudden droop-
ing and withering of her whole being, even the bangles on her
wrist slipping down, her attendants took her away and spread a
soft bed for her to lie on.

She lay tossing in her bed complaining, "You girls have for-
gotten how to make a soft bed. You are all out to tease me." Her
maids in attendance had never seen her in such a mood. They
were bewildered and amused at first, but later became genuinely
concerned, when they noticed tears streaming down her cheeks.
They found her prattling involuntarily, "Shoulders of emerald,
eyes like lotus petals, who is he? He invaded my heart and has
deprived me of all shame! A robber who could ensnare my heart
and snatch away my peace of mind! Broad-shouldered, but
walked off so swiftly. Why could he not have halted his steps, so
that I might have gained just one more glimpse and quelled this ri-
otous heart of mine? He was here, he was there next second, and
gone forever. He could not be a god—his eyelids flickered. . . . Or
was he a sorcerer casting a spell on people?"

The sun set beyond the sea, so says the poet—and when a poet mentions a sea, we have to accept it. No harm in letting a poet describe his vision, no need to question his geography. The cry of birds settling down for the night and the sound of waves on the seashore became clearer as the evening advanced into dusk and night. A cool breeze blew from the sea, but none of it comforted Sita. This hour sharpened the agony of love, and agitated her heart with hopeless longings. A rare bird, known as "Anril," somewhere called its mate. Normally at this hour, Sita would listen for its melodious warbling, but today its voice sounded harsh and odious. Sita implored, "Oh, bird, wherever you may be, please be quiet. You are bent upon mischief, annoying me with your cries and lamentations. The sins I committed in a previous birth have assumed your form and come to torture me now!" The full moon rose from the sea, flooding the earth with its soft light. At the sight of it, she covered her eyes with her palms. She felt that all the elements were alien to her mood and combining to aggravate her suffering. Her maids noticed her distress and feared that some deep-rooted ailment had suddenly seized her. They lit cool lamps whose wicks were fed with clarified butter, but found that even such a flame proved intolerable to her, and they extinguished the lamps and in their place kept luminous gems which emanated soft light. They made her a soft bed on a slab of moonstone with layers of soft petals, but the flowers wilted, Sita writhed and groaned and complained of everything— the night, stars, moonlight, and flowers: a whole universe of unsympathetic elements. The question went on drumming in her mind: "Who is he? Where is he gone? Flashing into view and gone again—or am I subject to a hallucination? It could not be so—a mere hallucination cannot weaken one so much."

At the guest house, Rama retired for the night. In the seclusion of his bedroom, he began to brood over the girl he had noticed on the palace balcony. For him, too, the moon seemed to emphasize his sense of loneliness. Although he had exhibited no sign of it, deeply within he felt a disturbance. His innate sense of discipline and propriety had made him conceal his feelings before other people. Now he kept thinking of the girl on the balcony and longed for another sight of her. Who could she be? Nothing to indicate that she was a princess—could be any one among the hundreds of girls in a palace. She could not be married: Rama realized that if she were married he would instinctively have recoiled from her. Now he caught himself contemplating her in every detail. He fancied that she was standing before him and longed to enclose those breasts in his embrace. He said to himself, "Even if I cannot take her in my arms, shall I ever get another glimpse, however briefly, of that radiant face and those lips? Eyes, lips, those curly locks falling on the forehead—every item of those features seemingly poised to attack and quell me— me, on whose bow depended the destruction of demons, now at the mercy of one* who wields only a bow of sugarcane and uses flowers for arrows . . ." He smiled at the irony of it.

The night spent itself. He had little sleep. The moon set and the dawn came. Rama found that it was time to arise and prepare himself to accompany his master to the ceremony at Janaka's palace.

At the assembly hall King Janaka noticed Rama and Lakshmana, and asked Viswamithra, "Who are those attractive-looking young men?" Viswamithra explained. When he heard of Rama's lineage and prowess, Janaka said with a sigh, "How I wish it were possible for me to propose my daughter for him." Viswamithra understood the cause of his despair. A seemingly insurmountable condition existed in any proposal concerning Sita's marriage.

King Janaka had in his possession an enormous bow which at one time belonged to Shiva, who had abandoned it and left it in the custody of an early ancestor of Janaka's, and it had remained an heirloom. Sita, as a baby girl, was a gift of Mother Earth to Janaka, being found in a furrow when a field was ploughed. Janaka adopted the child, tended her, and she grew up into a beauty, so much so that several princes who considered themselves eligible thronged Janaka's palace and contended for Sita's hand. Unable to favour anyone in particular, and in order to ward them off, King Janaka made it a condition

*Manmatha, the god of love.

that whoever could lift, bend, and string Shiva's bow would be considered fit to become Sita's husband. When her suitors took a look at the bow, they realized that it was a hopeless and unacceptable condition. They left in a rage, and later returned with their armies, prepared to win Sita by force. But Janaka resisted their aggression, and ultimately the suitors withdrew. As time passed Janaka became anxious whether he would ever see his daughter married and settled—since the condition once made could not be withdrawn. No one on earth seemed worthy of approaching Shiva's bow. Janaka sighed. "I tremble when I think of Sita's future, and question my own judgement in linking her fate with this mighty, divine heirloom in our house."

"Do not despair," said Viswamithra soothingly. "How do you know it was not a divine inspiration that gave you the thought?"

"In all the worlds, is there anyone who can tackle this bow, the very sight of which in Shiva's hand made erring gods and godlings tremble and collapse—until Shiva put it away and renounced its use?"

"With your permission, may we see it?"

Janaka said, "I'll have it brought here. It has lain in its shed too long. . . . Who knows, moving it out may change all our fates." He called on his attendants to fetch the bow. . . . The attendants hesitated and he ordered, "Let the army be engaged for the task if necessary. After all, this spot is sanctified by the sacred rites recently performed . . . and the bow is fit to be brought in here."

The bow was placed in a carriage on eight pairs of wheels and arrived drawn by a vast number of men. During its passage from its shed through the streets, a crowd followed it. It was so huge that no one could comprehend it at one glance. "Is this a bow or that mountain called Meru, which churned the Ocean of Milk in ancient times?" people marvelled. "What target is there to receive the arrow shot out of this bow, even if someone lifts and strings it?" wondered some. "If Janaka meant seriously to find a son-in-law, he should have waived this condition. How unwise of him!"

Rama looked at his master. Viswamithra nodded as if to say, "Try it." As Rama approached the bow with slow dignity, the onlookers held their breath and watched. Some prayed silently for him. Some commented, "How cruel! This supposed sage is not ashamed to put the delicate, marvellous youth to this harsh trial!" "The King is perverse and cruel to place this godlike youth in this predicament. . . . If he was serious about it, he should have just placed Sita's hand in his instead of demanding this acrobatic feat. . . ." "The King's aim is to keep Sita with him for ever—this is one way of never facing separation!" "If this man fails, we will all jump into fire," commented some young women who were love-stricken at the sight of Rama. "If he fails, Sita is sure to immolate herself and we will all follow her example."

While they were speculating thus, Rama approached the bow. Some of the onlookers, unable to bear the suspense, closed their eyes and prayed for his success, saying, "If he fails to bring the ends of this bow together, what is to happen to the maiden?" What they missed, because they had shut their eyes, was to note how swiftly Rama picked up the bow, tugged the string taut, and brought the tips together. They were startled when they heard a deafening report, caused by the cracking of the bow at its arch, which could not stand the pressure of Rama's grip.

The atmosphere was suddenly relaxed. The gods showered down flowers and blessings, clouds parted and precipitated rains, the oceans tossed up in the air all the rare treasures from their depths. The sages cried, "Janaka's tribulations and trials are ended." Music filled the air. The citizens garlanded, embraced, and anointed each other with perfumes and sprinkled sandalwood powder in the air. People donned their best clothes, gathered at the palace gates and public squares, and danced and sang without any restraint; flutes and pipes and drums created a din over the loud chants and songs from many throats. Gods and goddesses watching the happy scenes below assumed human form, mixed with the crowds, and shared their joy. "The beauty of our royal bridegroom can never be fully grasped unless one is blessed with a thousand eyes," commented the women. "See his brother! How very handsome! Blessed parents to have begotten such sons!"

Sita had secluded herself and was unaware of the latest development. She moved from bed to bed for lack of comfort, and lay beside a fountain on a slab of moonstone—the coolest bed they could find her. Even there she had no peace since the lotus blooms in the pool of the fountain teased her mind by reminding her of the shape of *his* eyes or *his* complexion. She grumbled, "No peace anywhere . . . I am deserted. My mind tortures me with reminders. What use are they if I can't even know where to look for him? What sort of a man can he be to cause all this torment and just pass on doing nothing to alleviate it? A regal appearance, but actually practising sorcery!"

Her tortuous reflections were interrupted by the arrival of a maid. Instead of bowing and saluting her mistress, as was normal, she pirouetted around singing snatches of a love song. Sita sat up and commanded, "Be quiet! Are you intoxicated?" The maid answered, "The whole country is intoxicated. How would you know, my good mistress, if you lock yourself in and mope and moan?" She went on to explain in a rush of incoherence. "The king of Ayodhya . . . son, broad-shouldered and a god on earth. No one saw it happen, he was so quick and swift, but he pressed, so they say, one end with his feet, and seized the other end with his hand, and drew the string and oh! . . ."

"Oh, intoxicated beauty, what are you saying?" When Sita understood what had happened, she stood up, her breasts heaving. She held herself erect as she said, "Do you know if this is the same man who struck me down with a look as he passed along the street? If it is someone else, I will end my life."

When the initial excitement subsided, King Janaka sought Viswamithra's advice. "What shall I do next? I suddenly find myself in an unexpected situation. Is it your desire that I should send for the priests and astrologer and fix the earliest date for the wedding, or send a message to Dasaratha and wait for his convenience?"

Viswamithra replied, "Dispatch a messenger with the auspicious news immediately and invite Dasaratha formally." Janaka at once retired in order to compose a proper invitation to Dasaratha, with the help of his court poets and epistle-writers, and dispatched it.

In due course, Janaka's emissaries presented the epistle at

Dasaratha's court. Dasaratha ordered his reader to receive the epistle and read it out: The message gave an account of all that had happened from the time Rama had left Ayodhya up to the snapping of Shiva's bow. Dasaratha heaped presents on the messengers, and commented light-heartedly, "Tell them in Mithila that we heard the sound of the bow snapping. . . ." He then passed orders: "Let the announcement in appropriate language be made widely that King Janaka has invited for Rama's wedding every man, woman, and child in our capital. Let those able to travel to Mithila start at once in advance of us." Professional announcers on elephants, accompanied with drums, carried the King's proclamation to every nook and corner of the capital.

The road to Mithila was crowded with men, women, and children. When the huge mass began to assemble and move down the road, the world looked suddenly shrunken in size. Elephants bearing pennants and flags, their foreheads covered with gold plates, horses prancing and trotting, and a variety of ox-drawn carriages and chariots were on the move, in addition to a vast throng on foot. The sun's rays were caught and reflected by the thousands of white satin umbrellas and the brilliant decorations of the army men. Heavy-breasted women clad in gossamer-like draperies sat on dark elephants, their necklaces swaying with the movement of the elephants, flanked by warriors bearing swords and bows on horseback.

The poet is especially happy and detailed when describing the mood and the activity of the young in this festive crowd. A youth followed a carriage at a trot, his eyes fixed on the window at which a face had appeared a little while ago, hoping for another glimpse of that face. Another young man could not take his eye off the lightly covered breast of a girl in a chariot; he tried to keep ahead of it, constantly looking back over his shoulder, unaware of what was in front, and bumping the hindquarters of the elephants on the march. When a girl inadvertently slipped down the back of a horse, another young man picked her up; but instead of setting her down after the rescue, he journeyed on with her in his arms. Another went along brooding and reflecting as he gazed on his beloved. Couples who had had a quarrel over some detail of the arrangements for this journey walked side by side without speaking, the woman not caring to wear a flower in her hair, but only a frown on her face, yet close enough to each other to avoid separation. One youth who was not spoken to but was agitated by the messages conveyed by the eloquent eyes of a damsel said, "You won't speak? But surely, when you cross the river, you'll want my strong arms to carry you, and how shall I know if you don't speak to me? I know that you object only to speech, not to my touch, inevitable you'll need that when we come to the river's edge."

Camels bearing enormous loads went along with parched throats until they could find the bitter *margosa* leaves—since they avoid tender greenery—and were thirsty again after chewing them, like men who look only for wine to quench their thirst, which again produces more thirst. Sturdy menfolk bore on their shoulders gifts and supplies for the journey.

Brahmins who practised austerities followed, remaining aloof, afraid alike to walk amongst the elephants, for fear of being jostled, and in the areas where there were women, who might distract their inner vision. Some hopped along lightly on their toes, in order not to trample on any live creature on the ground; others held their fingers over their nostrils, both to perform breath control and to keep the fingers from touching their nether portions while their minds were fixed on God.

The noise of the rolling chariot wheels, trumpets, and drums, and the general din, made it impossible for anyone to hear what anyone else was saying. After a while people moved along dumbly, communicating with each other only by signs, their feet raising an enormous trail of dust. Bullocks drawing wagons loaded with baggage, excited by the noise of drums, suddenly snapped off their yokes and ran helter-skelter, adding to the melee, leaving the baggage scattered on the road. Elephants, when they noticed a tank or a pond, charged away for a plunge, and remained submerged in the water up to their white tusks. Musicians sat on horseback playing their instruments and singing.

Behind this army, the king's favourites in the women's apartments followed. Surrounded by a thousand attendants, Queen

Kaikeyi came in her palanquin. Next came Sumithra, accompanied by two thousand attendants. Surrounded by her own musicians came Kausalya, mother of Rama. She had also in her company several dwarfs and hunchbacks and other freaks. But her main companions were sixty thousand women of great beauty and accomplishment who followed her in a variety of vehicles. In a white palanquin studded with pearls, sage Vasishtha, chief mentor at the court, followed, surrounded by two thousand brahmins and priests. Bharatha and Sathrugna, also younger brothers of Rama, came next. Dasaratha, after performing his daily duties and religious rites and presentation of gifts to brahmins, started to leave his palace at an auspicious conjunction of the planets, ushered by a number of priests, men bearing in their arms golden pots filled with holy waters which they sprinkled on his path, while several women recited hymns.

When the King emerged from his palace, many rulers from the neighbouring states were waiting to greet him. Conch and trumpets were sounded, and loud cheering and the recital of honours, when his carriage began to move.

After journeying for a distance of two *yojanas,* the King with his army and followers camped in the shadow of Mount Saila. Next day the camp moved on to a grove beside a river.

The forward portions of the advance party, which had already reached Mithila, were received and absorbed into homes, palaces, and camps in the capital. As further contingents kept coming in, they too were received. The line of movement was continuous from Ayodhya to Mithila. King Dasaratha's party was the last to arrive. When the scouts who watched for their arrival flew back on horses to report that Dasaratha's party had been sighted, Janaka went forth with his ministers and officials and guards of honour to receive him. The two kings met, greeted each other, exchanged polite formalities; then Janaka invited Dasaratha to get into his own chariot and proceeded towards the capital. While they were entering the gates of the city, Rama, accompanied by Lakshmana, met them, greeted his father, and welcomed him. Dasaratha swelled with pride at the sight of his son, whose stature seemed so much grander now.

At this point Kamban begins to describe the preparations for the wedding of Rama and Sita. It is one of the most fascinating sections of the epic. The details of the wedding pavilion; the decorations; the arrival of guests from other countries; the flowers and gaiety; the citizens' joy and participation; the activities in the bride's house and then at the bridegroom's, and the preparation of the bride and bridegroom themselves: their clothes and jewellery, the moods they were in—all are described by Kamban in minute detail, running to several thousand lines of poetry.

At an auspicious conjunction of the planets suitable to the horoscopes of Rama and Sita, in ceremonials conducted by the high priests of Mithila and Ayodhya in Janaka's court, Rama and Sita became man and wife.

"Those who were together only a little while ago came together again, and there was no need for any elaborate ritual of speech between them," says Kamban, describing the couple's first meeting at the conclusion of the wedding ceremonies.

Through Janaka's efforts, Rama's three brothers were also found brides and were married at the same time, in Mithila. When the celebrations ended, King Dasaratha started back for Ayodhya, with his sons bringing home their wives. On the day they left, Viswamithra told Dasaratha, "Now I return to you Rama and Lakshmana. Their achievements are immeasurable, but there is much more ahead. They are blessed men." Then he took leave of them and abruptly left northward. He was retiring into the Himalayas, away from all activities, to spend the rest of his days in contemplation.

3

TWO PROMISES REVIVED

In his busy life Dasaratha perhaps had never studied his mirror properly. He had had no occasion to scrutinize himself too long in the mirror or engage himself in any introspection. Suddenly one day he noticed the whitening hair and the wrinkles under his eyes—noticed the slight tremor of his hands, the fatigue of his legs while engaged in a game, and realized that age had come on. It was by no means inconsiderable. The original poet Valmiki mentions that Dasaratha was sixty thousand years old! In our modern reckoning we may not agree with that figure, but put it at sixty, seventy, or eighty years; whatever it was, ripeness is indicated.

In the loneliness of his chamber, Dasaratha told himself, "One must know when to cease, and not wait for death or dotage. While my faculties are intact, let me seek retirement and rest. There is no sense in continuing and repeating the same set of activities performed all these several thousand years, as it seems to me now. Enough, I have done enough. I must now find the time to stand back and watch and lay aside the burdens of office."

He arrived at a drastic decision. He summoned his aide to the door, and told him to summon Sumanthra, his chief minister, immediately. "Send round an announcement for all our officers and public men, sages and wisemen, and all our allies and kings and relations to gather at our hall of assembly. Let as many as possible arrive."

He added, while Sumanthra waited, "No need to inform, among our relatives, Aswapathi." He was the father of his third wife, Kaikeyi. Bharatha, her son, had gone there to spend a few days with his grandfather. "No need to trouble Janaka either. Mithila is too far away, and he will not be able to come in time."

"Is there anyone else to be omitted?"

"No. Invite as many as you can conveniently, and all our citizens." Messengers were dispatched in all directions. The assembly hall filled up. Dasaratha ascended the steps to his seat and, after the routine ceremonials, gestured to all to resume their seats, and spoke:

"I have performed my duties as King of this country long enough. Now I have an irresistible feeling that the burden must be shifted over to younger shoulders. What do you gentlemen think about it? Under the white umbrella of the royal state, apparently there has been no change—but actually the body under it is withering. I have lived and functioned long enough. If I still thought that I should continue thus endlessly, it would amount to avarice. The other day I realized that my signature on a document was hazy. My hand must have trembled without my knowing it. The time has come for me to sit back and rest—and anticipate the coming of grandchildren. If you will agree, I want to hand over the kingdom to Rama. He should be my successor, an embodiment of all perfection. He is perfect and will be a perfect ruler. He has compassion, a sense of justice, and courage, and he makes no distinctions between human beings—old or young, prince or peasant; he has the same consideration for everyone. In courage, valour, and all the qualities—none to equal him. He will be your best protector from any hostile force, be it human or subhuman or superhuman. His asthras, acquired from his master Viswamithra, have never been known to miss their mark. . . . I hope I shall have your support in anointing him immediately as the Emperor of Kosala."

A joyous shout rang through the assembly. Dasaratha waited for it to subside and asked, "I note the zest with which you welcome my successor. Should I take it that you do so because you have been bearing with me silently for any reason all these years, although I had thought I had dedicated my life fully to the welfare of my subjects?"

A spokesman rose and explained. "Do not mistake us, Your Majesty. It is our love for Rama that makes us so happy now. We have long looked forward to this moment. To see him ride the Royal Elephant in full paraphernalia through the streets of our capital is a vision of the future that we cherish, young and old alike, for we are lost in the splendour of Rama's personality. It is that anticipation that makes us applaud your proposal so unreservedly. It is not that we do not wish for the continuance of Your Majesty."

Dasaratha said, "I agree with you. I just wanted to know without a trace of doubt that you approve of my desire to make Rama your King. I desire that tomorrow when the *Pushya* star is in combination with the moon, and the time is auspicious, Rama be crowned."

He summoned his minister and the priest. "Let everything, every little detail be ready for the ceremony of coronation tomorrow. Let there be widespread decorations and have all items ready at the coronation hall. Let the streets be washed, cleaned, and decorated. Let people feast and play and enjoy themselves unlimitedly. Let there be arrangements to serve a feast continuously in every corner of this capital. . . ."

He sent for Rama. He watched his arrival from his balcony, received him warmly, took him aside, and said, "Tomorrow, you will be crowned as my successor. I need rest from work."

Rama accepted the proposal with a natural ease. Dasaratha continued. "You know everything, but still I feel it a duty to say a few words. You will have to pursue a policy of absolute justice under all circumstances. Humility and soft speech—there could be really no limit to these virtues. There can be no place in a king's heart for lust, anger, or meanness." He went on thus for some time and terminated the meeting. When Rama was back in his palace, explaining the situation to Sita, Sumanthra was once again knocking on his door.

"Your father summons you."

"Again? I have just come from him."

"He knows it, but wants you again."

When Rama presented himself, Dasaratha seated him and said, "You may be surprised at being called again. I am seized with anxiety that you should be crowned without any delay. I have premonitions which are frightening. I dream of comets, hear foul screeches from nowhere. I am told that my stars are not in a happy conjunction now. I dreamt that my star of nativity had crashed and was on fire. For one's proper birth, one owes a debt to the benediction of immortal sages, to one's ancestors, and to the gods; these three debts have to be discharged fully within the allotted span of one's life. I have no doubt that I have paid my debts fully by now. I have enjoyed my life, I have ruled as King with unquestioned authority and earned the love and confidence of my subjects. There is nothing left for me to do. I have grown old, my physical body is ready for dissolution. . . ."

He had said these things before and was now repeating himself. Rama understood that there must be some deep agitation within him. But out of respect and graciousness, he listened to it all again as if for the first time. "My stars, Mars and Jupiter, are aspecting the same house, so say my astrologers, which means death or near death or some catastrophe. And so I want to impress on you the urgency of the matter. Tomorrow's star will be Pushya, and the ceremony must be gone through, without doubts or impediments. Do not think for a moment that anything is postponable. Nothing should be put off, for we cannot say how fickle the human mind is, and what changes will occur therein. . . . And so what is important is that we should go through the ceremonies without hesitation. I want you to be very careful tonight, until the ceremony is over. Do not come out without your bodyguard, and observe all the austerities and vows to the last letter. Sita and yourself should have ritual baths and avoid your bed and sleep lightly on a mat of dharbha grass. . . . The ceremonies will begin at dawn. Be ready, and see that your robes are ready. You must fast tonight. Caution Sita not to delay. In a ceremonial, the wife's presence and timely participation are of the utmost importance. . . ."

Rama listened, promising to carry out every word of his instructions faithfully. Finally Dasaratha explained, "It is best to complete all this while Bharatha is away at his grandfather's place. It is good that he is away. I know his devotion to you, but the human mind, you know, can be fickle. . . . He may question why he should not have been the king . . . after all. But if he learns of it as an accomplished fact, I do not doubt that he will be extremely happy."

His father's deviousness was rather startling, but if he noticed it, Rama did not show it.

This worry at the back of Dasaratha's mind about Bharatha's claim turned out to be a valid one. Though Bharatha was away, his cause and claim were espoused by his mother Kaikeyi so energetically that it brought on disaster and changed the whole course of events in Rama's life. It came about thus. Kooni, a freak and hunchback (and nicknamed thus on account of her deformity), was the favourite of the King's favourite wife, Kaikeyi. On this particular day she climbed to the top terrace of Kaikeyi's mansion to view the city, and noticed the festoons and lights, and asked herself, "What are they celebrating today?"

When she went down, inquired, and found out the cause of the celebrations, she became excited, bit her lips, and muttered, "I will stop it." She hurried to Kaikeyi's chamber and shouted at her mistress, who was resting, "Is this the time to sleep? Wake up before you are ruined." Kaikeyi opened her eyes and cried, "You! Where have you been? What is troubling you?"

"Your impending fate," replied Kooni.

Kaikeyi was curious, but still without rising she said, "Kooni, something seems to be the matter with your health. Won't you call the physician and see that he sets you right?" She laughed and said, "Now calm down, sit near me, and sing me a song."

Kooni said sharply, "Do you know that beauty and youth are your only source of strength? And you owe your position as the queen of a world conqueror to your beauty?"

"Do I?" asked Kaikeyi, still in a playful mood.

"But both beauty and youth are like a wild stream, which, while rushing down the mountainside, crushing flowers and leaves, holds you in a spell. But how long does it last? Very soon it passes, and in its place you have only the sandy bed. . . . It's only a question of time. When you are old and the cheeks sag, you will be a nobody, pushed aside with the back of your lover's hand. You will be at other people's mercy."

"Bring that mirror, let me see why you speak thus. Have I grown old today?" And she laughed.

"Not old, but smug, and running into danger. Doom hangs over your head."

Now Kaikeyi felt disturbed. "If you cannot talk plainly, go away; and come later. You are somehow bent upon irritating me today."

"Don't waste your youth and beauty, which hold your husband in a spell. Before that's lost, get your husband to help you and save yourself. Get up and act before it's too late." Kaikeyi now sat up anxiously. Satisfied with the effect of her remarks, Kooni declared, "The King has cheated you. Tomorrow he is crowning Rama as the King of Ayodhya and retiring."

Kaikeyi got up, exclaiming, "Wonderful! Wonderful! Here is your reward for the good news you bear." She took off her necklace and threw it on Kooni's lap. Kooni received it and laid it aside. Now Kaikeyi said, "For the excellence of your news you deserve more. Tell me what you wish and you shall have it." This really provoked Kooni to cry out, "I said Rama is becoming the king of Ayodhya, and you behave as if I had said your son Bharatha . . ."

"I make no distinction between the two. It's all the same to me. Rama is the one who was born to it, and as a mother it makes me proud and happy. . . ."

"You, Rama's mother!"

"Yes, don't you know that one in Rama's position should count five mothers: the one who has borne him, a stepmother, a father's sister, an elder brother's wife, and the wife of the guru—all these have equal rank as mother. You understand why I feel happy about Rama? I adore him. I'm his mother as well as Kausalya is. And so make no mistake that I'm a fool and do not understand things!" At which Kooni beat her brow with her palms with such force that Kaikeyi said, "You have hurt yourself—a contusion big as my thumb!"

"I'd be happy if I killed myself or had not been born at all, rather than see all the treachery that goes on in this world," wailed Kooni. "My sorrow, now, is for you, the doom that overhangs you. It rends my heart to see the carefree innocence of your heart—it reminds me of the little dove flitting at the jaws of a wildcat."

All this amount of talk prepared Kaikeyi's mind to be receptive to what Kooni said next: "Your husband, the Emperor, is very cunning; he is capable of great trickery, unsuspected by you; great depths of trickery indeed, unbeknown to you, such depths as you cannot suspect even in your wildest dream. You and he are unequals. He was old enough to be your father when he asked for your hand; and your father refused the proposal, of course. But the old bridegroom was intoxicated with the spectacle of your beauty and youth, and was prepared to promise anything. He vowed to your father that he'd make the son borne by you the heir to the throne. I was the only one who overheard it. No one else knows about it. Now when the time came, the old man advised Bharatha sweetly: 'Why don't you go and spend a few days with your grandfather? He has been asking you so long.' And forthwith got him and his inseparable brother Sathrugna out of the way. He would have sent you away too—but for the fact that he can't survive even a single day without your caresses! Your charms are still potent. You will have to save yourself with their aid before it's too late. . . . Rama should not be enthroned tomorrow."

"Why not? The King may have his own reasons; and I see no difference between Rama and Bharatha."

"Do you know how people can change overnight? Tomorrow this time, he will be a different Rama. His only aim will be to stay long and strong in his seat, and to achieve it he will remove all hurdles. The chief hurdle will be Bharatha, who may assert his claim any time and win it by public support. Rama will banish him or break him down or behead him. You will no longer be a queen, but an ex-queen, of an ex-king, and will probably be reduced to the status of being the handmaid of the queen - mother Kausalya."

"Never! how would she dare!" cried Kaikeyi involuntarily. "Let her try!"

"By this time tomorrow, it could happen; it's bound to happen sooner or later." Thus Kooni had brought Kaikeyi to the brink of panic, before spelling out the remedy: "Do you remember

that Dasaratha was saved by you at one time, and there are two
ancient promises of his to be fulfilled? Leave alone his promise
to your father: you are not concerned with it. But hold on to the
two promises given to you. Demand first the banishment of
Rama to the forests for fourteen years, and secondly the crown-
ing of Bharatha in his place immediately."

"Impossible conditions; you must be drunk."

"No, quite practical, only go about it this way. . . ."

Thus it happened that when Dasaratha sought Kaikeyi's com-
pany, as was his wont, he did not find her in her chamber or the
garden. A maid told him, "She is in the *kopa gruha*."

"Why, why there?" He had had a tiring day. He had had
meetings again and again with his chief spiritual mentor, Va-
sishtha, and his chief minister, Sumanthra, going into details of
arrangements for the next day's ceremonials and festivities. "I
will be the host for the whole city tomorrow," he had said; "let
no one feel any want." Again and again he had mentioned how
every home and street and building should be decorated and
brightened; and how musicians, dancers, and entertainers
should be ready at the assembly hall before the dawn, and how
the state elephant and horses and chariots should move in the
procession of the newly crowned king; and named the streets
through which the procession should pass. "People would love
to see Rama on the throne and watch him in a procession.
Every man, woman, and child must have a chance to look at
him. Tell those conducting the procession to move slowly but
not so slowly as to tire Rama. . . ." He had gone into every de-
tail of the ceremonies. Exhausted, in the evening, he sought
Kaikeyi's company for relaxation.

He did not like the idea of being received by Kaikeyi in the
kopa gruha (the room of anger, which was a part of a dwelling
where one could retire to work off a bad mood); and when he
went in, he found her sprawling on the floor in semidarkness,
hair dishevelled, the flowers she had been wearing torn off, her
jewellery scattered, clad in indifferent clothes, and not noticing
his arrival. He stooped down to ask softly, "Are you unwell?"
She gave no answer to his question till he repeated it, and then

answered dully, "Oh, in perfect health, in every way. No physi-
cal sickness of any kind."

"I am sorry. I was delayed. I waited because I wanted to
bring you the news personally. I knew it would make you happy
indeed, and wanted to have the pleasure of watching your joy."

Kaikeyi condescended to mutter, "I knew it, I am not so stu-
pid or deaf or blind as not to know what is going on."

In that darkness and in the manner she had turned her face
down, he had no means of judging the mood in which she
spoke. It was difficult to be bending down so low, and he
pleaded, "Why don't you get up and sit on that couch, so that I
may sit beside you comfortably and listen to you?"

"You may seek all the comfort you want. I need none of it.
Dust and rags are my lot hereafter."

"What makes you talk in this manner? Get up and share the
happiness of the whole country. Let us drive around in your
chariot and see the joy that has seized the people."

"I want to be dead. That's all. If you could send me a bowl of
poison, that would be more welcome to me now." It was most
awkward for him to crouch or sit on the floor trying to appease
her. His joints ached and creaked. But she would not budge. It
was no time to call up an attendant, and so he pushed a foot-
stool beside her and lowered himself onto it. After a great deal
of cajoling, she announced: "Swear to me, by all that is holy,
that you will grant me what I ask for; otherwise let me die in
peace."

"I have never said no to you. You shall have whatever you
want."

"Will you swear by Rama?" she asked.

He evaded a direct answer, as he felt uneasy at the mention of
Rama's name. "Tell me what you want," he said clearly.

"You offered me two boons long ago. You may have forgot-
ten it, but I haven't. May I mention it now?" Now she had sat
up, and it was less irksome to communicate with her. He tried
to reach out and touch her, but she pushed his hand off. "On
that battlefield when you went to the rescue of Indra and
fainted, do you remember who revived you?"

"Yes," he said. "How can I forget it? I have lived to see this day because I was revived, otherwise that evening any chariot wheel could have rolled over me."

"Great memory you possess. I am glad you remember that far. And do you remember also who nearly gave her life to nurse and revive you?"

"Yes."

"What did you promise her in return?"

The king remained silent a moment, then said, "I have not forgotten."

"Bear with me if I repeat some small details that might escape your recollection. Let me help you. You said, 'Ask for two boons of your choice and you shall have them.' And then what did she do?" When he failed to answer, she added, "I said I would wait to take them, and you vowed, 'Whenever you like— even if it is a hundred years hence, you shall have whatever you ask for.'"

The King, who was becoming increasingly uneasy, simply said, "I see that the time has come for you to ask." There was no cheer in his tone. He was seized with dismal forebodings.

"Should I speak about it or not?"

"Get up and put on your festive clothes and jewellery so that you may shine like the resplendent star that you are. Let us go."

"Yes—in proper time—after you have fulfilled your promise to me." He had completely lost all courage to let her mention them. The sound of words such as "promise," "vow," "fulfill," "boon" shook his nerves. She looked up at him with tears in her eyes. He dared not look at her; he knew that he would be overwhelmed by her charms, and when she said presently, "Leave me now. Go back to your Kausalya and feast and enjoy. Leave me to myself." It was not necessary for her to mention "bowl of poison" again. He knew she meant it, and the prospect unnerved him. He said passionately, "You know how much I love you. Please, come out of this room and this mood."

"You have promised me the granting of two boons, and you have sworn to it in the name of Rama—your darling son Rama. And now I'll speak out my mind. If you reject my demand, you will be the first of the Ikshvahu race, proud descendents of the sun god himself, to go back on a promise for the sake of convenience." She took breath and demanded, "Banish Rama to the forests for fourteen years; and crown Bharatha and celebrate his enthronement with the arrangements you have already made."

The King took time to understand the import of this. He got up to his feet muttering, "Are you out of your mind? Or joking or testing me?" He moved away from her in search of the couch. He felt faint and blind, and groped about for a place to rest. He reclined on the couch and shut his eyes. She went on. "Send a messenger to fetch Bharatha at once. . . . He is quite far away. Give him time to come back. Tell Rama to take himself away."

"You are a demon," he whispered with his eyes still shut.

"Don't curse me, great King. I am not surprised that you find me less agreeable than Kausalya. Go on, go back to her and enjoy her company. I never asked you to come here and curse me. I retreated here just to avoid you."

The night continued in this kind of talk. Dasaratha made a last effort at compromise: "Very well, as you please. Let Bharatha be crowned. . . . But let Rama also stay here. You know him. He will hurt no one. Let Bharatha be the king by all means—he is good. But please, I'll touch your feet—I don't mind prostrating before you—but let Rama stay here in his own home and not go away. How can he walk those rough forest paths and go on living in the open, unsheltered . . . ?"

"He can, he is not the soft infant you make him out to be. For fourteen years he must live away, wear the bark of trees, eat roots and leaves. . . ."

"Do you want him to die . . . ? Ah . . ." The King screamed.

She merely said, "Don't create a scene. Either you keep your word or you don't, that's all."

The night spent itself in dead silence. Kaikeyi stayed where she was on the floor; the King lay on the couch. No one interrupted them. It was customary not to disturb when the King was with one of his wives. Even servants kept themselves out. For all that, it was inevitable that the King should be sought out

sooner or later. There were many matters on which he had to be
consulted. His chief minister was at his wit's end. "Where is the
King? Where is the King?" was the constant question.

The assembly hall was growing crowded with distinguished
guests and the public who thronged in to watch the corona-
tion. Rama, clad in simple silk robes after several ritual baths
and purification ceremonies ordained by the chief priest, was
also ready, waiting for the ceremonial dress. A little before the
dawn, the holy fire was lit in which offerings were to be placed
to please the gods in heaven. The priestly groups were already
chanting the sacred mantras in unison. Music from many
sources filled the air. The babble of the crowd was continuous.
But in the inner ring where the chief minister and other imme-
diate executives were assembled, there was concern. "The King
should have arrived by now. He must initiate the rites; he has
to receive the rulers who will soon be arriving. . . ." The chief
minister, Sumanthra, got up to find out the reason for the de-
lay. Things had to go according to a time-table in every detail
so as to synchronize with the auspicious movement of the
stars. And any single item delayed would throw the entire cer-
emony out of gear. Sumanthra left the assembly hall and went
in search of the King. He hesitated for a moment at the door of
the kopa gruha, but parted the curtains, opened the door, and
entered. The sight before him, naturally, startled him. "Is His
Majesty unwell?" asked the minister. "Asks him yourself,"
replied Kaikeyi.

"Are you also unwell? Has some food disagreed with you
both?" asked the minister anxiously. The queen gave him no
answer. The minister softly approached the couch and whis-
pered, "They are waiting for you. Are you ready to come to the
assembly?" The King stirred lightly and said, "Tell them all to
go back. It's all over. I have been trapped by a demon." Kaikeyi
now interposed to explain: "The King has strained himself and
has become incoherent. Go and send Rama."

Rama arrived, expecting his stepmother to bless him before
the ceremonies. At the sight of him Dasaratha cried out:
"Rama!" and lapsed into speechlessness. His appearance and

behaviour made Rama anxious. "Have I done something to up-set him? Any lapse in my duties or performance?"

Kaikeyi said, "I'll speak on his behalf; he finds it difficult to say it. Your coronation will not take place today." And then she specified in unambiguous terms what she expected of him. She told all about the original vow and the circumstances that led to it. "It is your duty to help your father fulfill his promise. Other-wise he will be damning himself in this and other worlds. You owe him a duty as his son."

Rama took in the shock, absorbed it within himself, and said, "I will carry out his wishes without question. Mother, be as-sured that I will not shirk. I have no interest in kingship, and no attachments to such offices, and no aversion to a forest exis-tence."

"Fourteen years," she reminded him.

"Yes, fourteen years. My only regret is that I have not been told this by my father himself. I would have felt honoured if he had commanded me directly."

"Never mind, you can still please him by your action. Now leave at once, and he will feel happy that you have acted with-out embarrassing him."

"I want you to assure him that I am not in the least pained by this order. I will take your word as his." He saw his father's plight and moved closer.

Kaikeyi said, "I will attend to him. Don't waste your time. You must leave without delay. That's his wish."

"Yes, yes, I'll do so. I will send a messenger to fetch Bharatha without any delay."

"No, no," said Kaikeyi. "Do not concern yourself with Bharatha. I'll arrange everything. You make haste to depart first." She knew Bharatha's devotion to Rama and, uncertain as to how he would react, preferred to have Rama well out of the way before Bharatha should arrive. "I'll take leave of my mother, Kausalya, and leave at once," said Rama. He threw another look at his speechless father and left.

When Rama emerged from Dasaratha's palace, a crowd was waiting to follow him to the assembly hall. Looking at his face, they found no difference on it, but instead of ascending the chariot waiting for him, he set out on foot in the direction of his mother's palace. They followed him.

Rama went up to his mother, Kausalya. She was weak with her fasts and austerities undertaken for the welfare of her son. She had been expecting him to arrive in full regalia but noted the ordinary silks which he wore and asked, "Why are you not dressed yet for the coronation?"

"My father has decided to crown Bharatha as the King," Rama said simply.

"Oh, no! But why?"

Rama said, "For my own good, my father has another command; it is for my progress and spiritual welfare."

"What is it? What can it be?"

"Only that for twice seven years, he wants me to go away and dwell in the forests, in the company of saints, and derive all the benefit therefrom."

Kausalya broke down and sobbed. She wrung her hands, she felt faint in the depth of her bowels, sighed, started out to say things but swallowed back her words. She said bitterly, "What a grand command from a father to a son!" She asked, "When do you have to go? What offence have you committed?"

Rama lifted his mother with his hands and said, "My father's name is renowned for the steadfastness of his words. Would you rather that he spoke false? . . . I am thrice blessed, to make my brother the King, to carry out my father's command, and to live in the forests. Do not let your heart grieve."

"I cannot say, 'Disobey your father,' only let me go with you. I cannot live without you."

"Your place is beside your husband. You will have to comfort and nurse him. You must see that he is not sunk in sorrow by my exile. You cannot leave him now. Also, later, my father may want to engage himself in the performance of religious rites for his own welfare, and you will be needed at his side. After living in the forests, I will come back—after all, fourteen years could pass like as many days. If you remember, my earlier stay in the forests with Viswamithra brought me countless blessings; this could be a similar opportunity again, for me. So do not grieve."

Kausalya now realized that Rama could not be stopped. She

thought, "Let me at least beg my husband's help to hold him back from this resolve. . . ." However, when she reached the King's chamber and saw his condition, she realized the hopelessness of her mission. As he lay there stunned and silent, she understood that he must be in some dreadful dilemma. Unable to bear the spectacle of an inert, lifeless husband, she uttered a loud wail. Her cries were so loud that the guests in the assembly hall were startled, and requested Sage Vasishtha to go up immediately and find out the cause. All kinds of music, chanting of hymns, prayers, laughter, and talk had filled the air; but this sudden intrusion of wailing destroyed the atmosphere of joy. Vasishtha hurried on. He found the King looking almost dead, Kaikeyi sitting apart and watching the scene unperturbed, and Kausalya in a state of complete desperation and wretchedness. He quickly tried to estimate the situation. It would be no use questioning Kausalya. He turned to the calm and firm-looking Kaikeyi. "Madam, what has happened?"

"Nothing to warrant all this hullaballoo," Kaikeyi said. "A situation like this ought to be ignored, a purely domestic matter. Do not be perturbed, sir. Go back to the assembly and tell them to be calm. A few changes in the arrangements, that's all. They will be told about it soon."

"I want to know everything," said Vasishtha emphatically.

She hastened to say, "Of course, you are our spiritual mentor and guide and you have every right to demand an explanation." While she spoke, Vasishtha saw Kausalya writhing and squirming, and Dasaratha stirring. Dasaratha was evidently aware of what was going on in the room though unable to take part in the conversation. Lest either of them should begin to say things at cross-purposes with her, Kaikeyi said, "Your wisdom sustains us, sir. You will realize that nothing untoward has happened. Before I had even spoken fully, Rama understood and agreed. It's the others who are making all this fuss. Rama has surrendered his right to the throne in favour of Bharatha, and will stay away in the forest for fourteen years. It's a thing that concerns primarily himself, and he has accepted it without a word, with much grace. But these others think . . ." She swept her arm to indicate several hostile persons.

Vasishtha understood, but still asked, "What is the cause of this change?"

Kaikeyi, whose good manners had reached their limit, now said, "If my husband will speak, he can—otherwise please wait. Just tell those assembled that there is a change in the programme."

"That we will see later," said Vasishtha. "First we must revive the King." He stooped over the King lying on the couch, gently lifted his head, and helped him to sit up. "We need you, Your Majesty. You are our lord and captain. What is to happen if you are withdrawn like this?"

The King went on mumbling, "Kaikeyi, Kaikeyi . . ."

Vasishtha said, "The Queen, Kaikeyi, is most considerate. She will do nothing that goes against your wishes. I am sure she will be obliging and helpful. There has been no opportunity to discuss these questions with her Majesty, our immediate concern being your welfare." Kaikeyi listened passively to this hopeful statement by Vasishtha.

Dasaratha, clutching at a straw of hope, asked, "Does she relent? If she does, Rama will be King; and as to my promise, let her ask for any other fulfillment she may think of. . . ."

Relieved to find the King improving, Vasishtha turned to Kaikeyi and appealed to her with all the humility he could muster in his tone. "Everything is in your hands. . . . Please consider yourself as the benefactress of humanity. The whole world will be grateful to you for your help. Please reconsider."

Kaikeyi became emotional: "If one cannot depend on the promise of a famous king," she hissed, "life is not worth living. After all, I have done nothing more than ask for the fulfillment of his own voluntary promise, and you talk as if I had committed a crime!"

"You do not realize the evil consequences of your act, nor are you willing to listen and understand when we try to explain. Your obstinacy is inhuman," said Vasishtha. When she appeared unaffected, he went on: "The King's tongue never uttered the words of exile; you have passed this on as his own command, knowing that Rama would never question the truth of it. You have used your position as his favourite queen."

No matter how he argued and persuaded, Kaikeyi held her ground with cynical calm. "Oh, Guruji, you too talk like these ignorant, self-centered people who find fault with me without understanding."

Finally the King burst out, "Oh, devilish one, you ordered him into exile! Is he gone? In seeking you as a mate, I sought my death. Those cherry-red lips I thought sustained me, but they have only been a source of the deadliest poison to finish me off now. This sage be my witness. You are no longer my wife, and your son shall not be entitled to cremate me when I die."

Kausalya, when she saw her husband's plight, was most moved and tried to comfort him in her own way. Concealing her own misery at the prospect of Rama's exile, she told her husband clearly, "If you do not maintain the integrity and truth of your own words, and now try to hold Rama back, the world will not accept it. Try to lessen your attachment to Rama and calm yourself."

The King was not appeased by her advice. "The holy water from Ganga brought for ablution during the coronation will now serve me for my last drink; the holy fire raised will serve to light my funeral pyre. Rama, Rama, don't go. I take back my word to Kaikeyi. . . . How can I bear to see you go? I will not survive your departure. If I lived after your departure, what would be the difference between me and that monster in wife's shape— Kaikeyi?" Thus and in many other ways, Dasaratha lamented.

Vasishtha said, "Do not grieve. . . . I will see that your son is persuaded to stay back." Dasaratha had become so weakened in will that he clung to this hope when he saw the sage depart. Kausalya comforted the King by saying, "It is quite likely Vasishtha will come back with Rama." She tenderly lifted him, nursed him, and stroked his head and shoulder. He kept repeating, "Will Rama come? When? How terrible that Kaikeyi, whom I loved so much, should contrive my death so that she may place Bharatha on the throne!" Silence for a while, but once again all his lamentations and fears would return redoubled.

"Kausalya, my dearest wife, listen. Rama will not change his aim, but definitely go away, and my life will end. You know why? It's an old story.

"Once while I was hunting in a forest, I heard the gurgling of water—the noise an elephant makes when drinking water. I shot an arrow in that direction, and at once heard a human cry in agony. I went up and found that I had shot at a young boy. He had been filling his pitcher; and water rushing into it had created the noise. The boy was dying and told me that his old parents, eyeless, were not far away. He had tended them, carrying them about on his back. They died on hearing of this tragedy, after cursing the man who had killed their son to suffer a similar fate. And so that is going to be my fate. . . ."

When Rama's exile became known, the kings and commoners assembled at the hall broke down and wept; so did the religious heads and ascetics. Men and women wept aloud; the parrots in their cages wept, the cats in people's homes; the infants in their cradles, the cows and calves. Flowers that had just bloomed wilted away. The water birds, the elephants, the chargers that drew chariots—all broke down and lamented like Dasaratha himself, unable to bear the pang of separation from Rama. What a moment ago had been a world of festivities had become one of mourning. Crowds thronged hither and thither, stood in knots at street corners, watched the portals of the palace, speculating and commenting. "Kaikeyi—the red-lipped prostitute," they said. "We never suspected that our King was so lost in infatuation. . . . We thought that the red-lipped woman was our Queen, but she has shown her true nature—  using her flesh to bait a senile male, who has sought his own ruin and thereby the ruin of our country. Let Kaikeyi try and rule this country with her son—there will be none left to rule over; we will all kill ourselves or move out with Rama. Ah, unfortunate earth not destined to have Rama as your overlord! What is Lakshmana doing? How will he stand this separation? What justification can there be for breaking a promise made to Rama? Strange act of justice this! The world has suddenly gone mad!"

Lakshmana, on hearing of the developments, was roused like the fire starting to consume the earth on the last day. "Food kept for the lion is sought to be fed to the street puppy—so plans that doe-eyed Kaikeyi," commented Lakshmana. He picked up his sword and bow, put on his battle dress, and aggressively roamed the streets swearing, "Rama shall be crowned, and whoever comes in the way will be annihilated. Let the whole world come, I'll destroy everyone who opposes, and pile up their carcasses sky high. I'll seize the crown and will not rest till I place it on Rama's head. This I'll achieve this very day, this very day." Seeing his fiery eyes and hearing his stentorian challenges, people withdrew from his proximity. "If all the gods in heaven, all the demons, all the good people of the earth, and bad—if the whole world oppose me, I'll not relent or yield to the desire of a mere female. . . ."

His challenges and the rattling of his arms and the twanging of his bow-string reached the ears of Rama, who was just on his way to take leave of his stepmother Sumithra, Lakshmana's mother, and he immediately turned back and confronted Lakshmana. "What makes you wear all this battle-dress, and against whom are you uttering your challenges? And why are you so wild and angry?"

Lakshmana said, "If this is not the occasion for anger, when else is it? After having promised you your rightful place—to deny it now! I can't tolerate it. The vicious dreams of that black-hearted woman shall not be fulfilled. I'll not let my senses watch this injustice passively. I'll resist it till I perish."

"It was my mistake," said Rama. "I have only myself to blame for accepting my father's offer of the throne so readily without thinking of the consequences. Your tongue, learned in the recital of Vedas and all the truths of godly life, should not be allowed to utter whatever it likes so irresponsibly. Your charges will not stand the scrutiny of judicious and serene temperaments. You must not utter such bitter remarks about people who after all are none other than your father and mother." (Rama makes no distinction between mother and stepmother). "Calm yourself. Sometimes a river runs dry, and then it cannot be said to be the fault of the river—it's dry because the heavens are dry. So also, our father's change of mind, or the apparent hardheartedness of Kaikeyi, who has been so loving and kind, or Bharatha's chance of succession. . . . These are really not our own doing, but some higher powers have decreed them. Fate . . ."

"I'll be the fate to overpower fate itself," said Lakshmana, with martial arrogance. Rama argued with him further. "I'll change and alter fate itself, if necessary," repeated Lakshmana and concluded his sentence with the refrain, "Whoever dares to oppose my aim will be destroyed.

"I know no father and no mother, other than you," said Lakshmana, still unsoftened. "You are everything to me. And there is no meaning in my existence, and in the possession of my limbs and sense intact, unless I establish you on the throne as your right, irrespective of what a female serpent has tried to do. My blood boils and will not calm down—you will now see what my bow can do. . . ."

At this Rama held his hand back. He said, "I am firmly convinced that our mother Kaikeyi is the one who deserves to inherit this kingdom, having saved our father's life and being assured of his gratitude; it is Bharatha's privilege—being the one chosen by Kaikeyi; and my privilege is renunciation and the association of enlightened hermits of the forests. Do you want to let your anger rage until you have vanquished an innocent brother who has no part in this, a mother who has nursed us, and a father who was the greatest ruler on earth? Is that victory worth all this? Is this anger, which seeks to destroy all firm relationships, worth nurturing? Control yourself, and take your hand off your bow."

Lakshmana relaxed, muttering, "What's all this strength of my arm worth! Mere burden, if it cannot be employed to destroy evil when I see it; and my anger itself has now proved futile."

Rama went up with Lakshmana to bid farewell to his step-mother Sumithra. As had happened with the others, Sumithra also bewailed Rama's exile and tried to stop him. Once again, untiringly, Rama expressed his determination to go and his joy at being able to fulfill his father's terms. While they were talking, a servant maid sent by Kaikeyi came bearing in her arms garments made of tree barks, a reminder for Rama to change quickly and depart. Lakshmana ordered another set for himself,

shed the finery he was wearing, and changed into coarse bark.
Presently Rama, dressed like an ascetic or penitent, was ready
to leave. At the sight of his departure, the women wept. Rama
made one last attempt to leave Lakshmana behind but Laksh-
mana followed him stubbornly. He then went into Sita's cham-
ber and found her already dressed in the rough tree fibre—her
finery and jewels discarded and laid aside, although she had
decorated and dressed herself as befitting a queen a little while
ago. Rama, though he had been of so firm a mind for himself,
felt disturbed at the sight of her—the change being so sudden.
He said, "It was never my father's intention to send you along
with me. This is not the life for you. I have only come to take
your leave, not to take you with me. . . ."

"I'm dressed and ready, as you see. . . ."

"If it is your wish to discard fine clothes because I wear none,
you may do so, though it's not necessary."

"I'm coming with you; my place is at your side wherever you
may be. . . ."

Rama saw the determination in her eyes and made one last
plea. "You have your duties to perform here, my father and
mother being here. I'll be with you again."

"After fourteen years! What would be the meaning of my ex-
istence? I could as well be dead. It will be living death for me
without you. I am alive only when I am with you; a forest or a
marble palace is all the same to me."

When he realized that she could not be deflected from her
purpose, Rama said, "If it is your wish, so let it be. May the
gods protect you."

A large crowd had gathered outside the palace when Rama,
Lakshmana, and Sita emerged in their austere garb, as decreed
by Kaikeyi. Many wept at the sight of them, and cursed
Kaikeyi again and again among themselves. A silence en-
sued as Vasishtha arrived with every sign of urgency. The
crowd watched expectantly, a spurt of hope welling up in their
hearts of a last-minute development which could transform the
scene magically. For the first time people saw the sage Va-
sishtha looking forlorn and tired. Stepping up before Rama, he

said, "Do not go. The King desires you to stay and come back
to the palace."

"It is his desire I should be away. . . ."

"Not his. He never said it, it is your stepmother's order. She
has . . ."

Rama did not want him to continue his comment on Kaikeyi
and interrupted. "Forgive me. It is my duty to obey her also,
since she derives her authority from my father, and he has given
her his word. How can it be different now?"

"Your father is deeply grieving that you are leaving him. He
may not survive the separation, in his present state. . . ."

Rama said, "You are our teacher in all matters. Please com-
fort my father, see that he realizes the nature of our present
situation—of my duty as his son in keeping his word. A word
given is like an arrow, it goes forward. You cannot recall it mid-
way. . . ." He made a deep bow to indicate that he had nothing
more to say. Vasishtha turned back without a word, and with-
drew, unwilling to be seen with tears in his eyes.

When Rama took a step, the whole crowd stepped forward,
and it stopped when he stopped. No one spoke. Considering
the vastness of the crowd, the silence was overwhelming. There
were tears in several eyes. Rama told someone nearest to him,
"Now, I'll take leave of you all," and brought his palms to-
gether in a salutation. They returned the salutation, but moved
when he moved, showing not the least sign of staying back.
They surrounded Rama, Sita, and Lakshmana. The crowd was
suffocating. After they had proceeded along for some distance,
the crowd made way for a chariot which pulled up. Sumanthra
got out of it and said, "Get into the chariot. Sita Devi may not
be able to walk through this crowd. . . ."

Rama smiled to himself. "She has undertaken to keep me
company and may have to go a long way on foot yet."

"Still, when a chariot is available, please come. At least you
can leave the crowd behind and get ahead. . . ."

Rama helped Sita up into the chariot. The horses started to
gallop, but not too far—to no purpose actually, as the crowd
made it difficult for the vehicle to proceed except at a walking
pace. Rama said, "Let us go slowly; no harm." Lakshmana

added, "Our stepmother has at least refrained from specifying how fast you should get away!"

They reached the banks of the river Sarayu and camped there for the night. The citizens who had followed also spread themselves out on the sand, not in the least minding the discomfort. Past midnight, fatigued by the trekking, the whole gathering had gone off to sleep. Rama said softly to Sumanthra, "This is the time to leave. You may go back to the palace and tell my father that I am safe." While the followers slept, Rama, Sita, and Lakshmana rode out to a farther point on the river, crossed it, and went up the embankment. Sumanthra watched them go and then turned back, following Rama's suggestion that he should reach the capital by another route without waking the crowd.

Dasaratha lay inert, motionless, with his eyes closed—except when a footstep sounded outside, at which time his lips moved as he whispered, "Has Rama come?" When Vasishtha or Kausalya gave some soothing answer, he lapsed into his drowsy state again. "Who is gone to fetch him?"

"Sumanthra," Vasishtha replied. Finally a footstep did sound, loudly enough to rouse the drowsy King. The door opened, and the King also opened his eyes and exclaimed, "Ah, Sumanthra? Where is Rama?" Before Vasishtha or Kausalya could prevent his reply, Sumanthra explained, "Rama, Sita and Lakshmana crossed the river, went up the bank, and then along a foot track that wound its way through a cluster of bamboos. . . ."

"Oh!" groaned the King. "How, how . . . When?" He could not complete the sentence. Sumanthra tried to say, "Rama wanted to escape the crowd. . . ."

The thought of Rama and Sita on the rough forest track beyond bamboo clusters was too unbearable for Dasaratha. He fell into a swoon and never recovered from the shock. ("He died even as Sumanthra was speaking," says the poet.)

The King's death left the country without a ruler for the time being. Vasishtha convened an urgent council of the ministers and

officials of the court and decided, "The first thing to do is to pre-
serve the King's body until Bharatha can come back and perform
the funeral." They kept the body embalmed in a cauldron of oil.

Two messengers were dispatched with a sealed packet for
Bharatha, advising him to return to the capital urgently. The
messengers were to keep their horses continously at a gallop,
and were not to explain anything or convey any information.
They were trusted men, experienced in the task of carrying
royal dispatches, and could be depended upon not to exceed
their orders. Within eight days, they drew up at the portals of
Aswapathi's palace at Kekaya and declared, "We carry an im-
portant message for Bharatha."

Bharatha was overjoyed, and ordered, "Bring them up with
the least delay." He received them in his chamber and asked at
once, "Is my father happy and in good health?" The messengers
murmured a polite answer, and Bharatha, "How is my brother,
Rama?" And they repeated their polite murmuring again, and
said, "We bear an epistle for Your Highness." Bharatha re-
ceived the sealed message (written on palm leaf and wrapped in
silk), opened it, and read: "Your return to Ayodhya is urgently
required in connection with state affairs." He ordered that the
message bearers be rewarded liberally and began immediate
preparations for his return to Ayodhya, without having the pa-
tience even to consult the palace astrologer as to the propitious
time for starting on a long journey.

When they reached the outskirts of Ayodhya, Bharatha
asked his brother Sathrugna, "Do you notice any change in the
atmosphere?"

"No traffic of chariots or horse-riders, no spectacle of people
moving about in public squares and highways . . ."

"Streets and homes without any illumination."

"No sound of music—no happy voices or songs or instru-
ments . . . What oppressive silence! So few to be seen in the
streets, and even the one or two we meet look up with such un-
smiling faces! What is wrong with them?"

Bharatha drove straight to Dasaratha's palace, went up, and
burst into his chamber with words of greeting on his lips. Not
finding the King in his usual place, he paused, wondering where

he should seek him. Just then an inner door opened, a maid appeared and said, "Your mother summons you." Immediately he left for Kaikeyi's apartment. He made a deep obeisance to her, touched her feet, and Kaikeyi asked, "Are my father, brothers, and the others safe and happy in Kekaya?"

Bharatha replied that all was well in her father's home. He then asked, "I want to touch the lotus feet of my father. Where is he gone? Where can I seek him?"

"The great King has been received by resplendent heavenly beings in the next world. He is happy and at peace. Do not grieve," replied Kaikeyi calmly.

When he took in the full import of her news and found his tongue again, Bharatha said, "None but you could have uttered these terrible words in this manner. Is your heart made of stone? I should never have left his side. My misfortune, my mistake. The world has not seen a greater ruler; no son has had a nobler father. I was not fated to be with him, to hear his voice, to feel his glorious presence—enjoying my holiday indeed! What a time to have chosen for relaxation!" He recounted again and again his father's exploits as a warrior, and this in some measure mitigated his anguish. After a long brooding silence he said, "Until I see Rama and listen to his voice, my grief will not abate."

At this point, Kaikeyi said in a matter-of-fact voice, "With his wife and brother, he left to live in the forests."

"What a time to have chosen for forest-going! When will he be back? What made him go? Did he go there before the King's death or after? Has he committed a wrong? What could be the cause of his exile, if it is an exile? Did the gods decree it or the King? Did he go before or after the King's death? Oh, impossible thought—did he commit a wrong? But if Rama committed a seemingly wrong act, it would still be something to benefit humanity, like a mother forcibly administering a medicine to her child."

"It's none of what you think. He went away with the full knowledge of your father."

"My father dies, my brother is exiled. . . . What has happened? What is all this mystery? What is behind all this?"

"Now attend to what I am going to say, calmly and with good sense. Of course, it would have been splendid if your father had lived. But it was not in our hands. You will have to accept things as they come and not let your feelings overpower and weaken your mind. Through your father's irrevocable promise to grant me two wishes, you are today lord of this earth, and Rama has willingly removed himself from your path. After he gave me his promise, your father became rather weak in mind. . . ."

Bharatha understood now. He ground his teeth, glared at her and thundered, "You are a serpent. You are heartless. You have had the cunning, the deviousness, to trap the King into a promise, and not cared that it meant death to him. How am I to prove to the world that I have no hand in this? How can anyone help thinking that I have manoeuvered it all through? . . . You have earned me the blackest reputation for anyone since the beginning of our solar race."

He concluded with regret, "You deserve to die for your perfidy. . . . If I do not snuff your wretched life out with my own hand, do not pride yourself that it is because you are my mother, but you are spared because Rama would despise me for my deed."

He left her without another word and went off sobbing to the palace of Kausalya, Rama's mother. She received him with all courtesy and affection, although she could not be quite clear in her mind about Bharatha's innocence. Bharatha threw himself before her and lamented, "In which world shall I seek my father? Where can I see my brother again? Have the fates kept me away in my grandfather's house so that I may suffer this pang?"

After he had gone on thus for some time expressing his sorrow and his determination to destroy himself rather than bear the burden of both separation and ill-repute, Kausalya realized that Bharatha was innocent. She asked at the end of his speech, "So you were unaware of the evil designs of your mother?"

At this Bharatha was so incensed that he burst into self-damnation: "If I had the slightest knowledge of what my mother was planning, may I be condemned to dwell in the darkest hell reserved for . . ." And he listed a series of the blackest sins for which people were committed to hell.

Vasishtha arrived. Bharatha asked, "Where is my father?" He was taken to where the King's body was kept.

Vasishtha said, "It is time to go through the funeral rites." When Bharatha was ready for the ceremonies, Dasaratha's body was carried in a procession on elephant back to the accompaniment of mournful drums and trumpets, to the bank of the Sarayu River, where a funeral pyre had been erected. Dasaratha's body was laid on it with elaborate prayers and rituals. When the time came to light the pyre, Bharatha approached it with a flame in his hand; suddenly, at the last moment, Vasishtha stopped him, remembering Dasaratha's last injunction disowning Kaikeyi and her son. He explained it delicately and with profound sorrow: "The most painful duty that the gods have left me to perform."

Bharatha understood. He withdrew, leaving his brother Sathrugna to continue the performance, with the bitter reflection, "This again my mother's gift to me, not even to be able to touch my father's funeral pyre!"

At the end of the day, Bharatha retired to his palace and shut himself in. After five days of mourning, the ministers and Vasishtha conferred, approached Bharatha, and requested him to become their King, as the country needed a ruler. Bharatha refused the suggestion and announced, "I am determined to seek Rama and beg him to return." He ordered that all citizens and the army should be ready to accompany him to the forest. A vast throng of citizens, army, horses, elephants, women, and children, set forth in the direction of Chitrakuta, where Rama was camping. Bharatha wore a garment made of tree bark, and insisted on accomplishing the journey on foot as a penance, following Rama's own example. When they crossed the Ganges and came within sight of Chitrakuta, Lakshmana, who had set himself as Rama's bodyguard, noticed the crowd at a distance and cried out, "There he comes, with an army—to make sure that you don't return to claim his ill-gotten kingdom. I'll destroy the whole lot. I have enough power in my quiver."

While they stood watching, Bharatha left his followers behind and came forward alone in his tree-bark garb, his arms held aloft in supplication, with tears in his eyes, praying, "Rama,

Rama, forgive me." Rama whispered to Lakshmana, "Do you note his martial air, and the battle-dress he has put on?"

Lakshmana hung his head and confessed, "I had misjudged him."

Bharatha flung himself down at Rama's feet. Rama lifted him up with many kind words.

When Rama learned of his father's death, he broke down. After a while, when he recovered, he set about performing on the river bank the rites required of the son of the departed King. When they settled down after the ceremonies, Bharatha opened the subject. "I have come with all these people to beg you to return home and be our King."

Rama shook his head and said, "Yes, fourteen years hence. That was our father's wish. You are the King by his authority."

"If you think I should be the King, so be it, but I abdicate this instant, and crown you."

The argument went on at a highly academic and philosophical level, the entire assembly watching with respect.

In a world where we are accustomed to rivalries over possession, authority, and borders, and people clashing over the issue, "Ours," or "Mine, not yours," it is rather strange to find two people debating whose the kingdom is *not*, and asserting: "Yours, not mine."

"So be it; if I have the authority—then I confer it on you as the ruler," said Bharatha at one stage. "On my command as the ruler, if you desire to think so, you shall be the King." It went on thus. Rama went on repeating that there could be no word higher than that of a father; no conduct other than obedience to it. Throughout he referred to Kaikeyi in the gentlest terms and always as "mother." Vasishtha, watching the debate, burst out: "I have been your guru; there can be no higher authority than a guru—you must return to Ayodhya as King." Rama said, "It's not right to give me that command. My parents, who have given me my body and mind, are higher than a guru."

Bharatha declared, "This is my vow. I don't care what happens. I shall renounce everything and live in the forest with Rama for fourteen years."

The gods watched this argument, afraid that if Rama returned to the kingdom, overwhelmed by the needs of the country, the purpose of his incarnation would be defeated, and proclaimed: "Bharatha, go back and rule on Rama's behalf for fourteen years."

There was nothing more to it. Bharatha said, "I have nothing more to say. I shall rule for fourteen years. But not a day longer. If you, Rama, do not appear at the end of fourteen years, I shall immolate myself. Give me your sandals, please. They will be your symbol, and I shall rule on behalf of that symbol. I will not re-enter Ayodhya until you come back, but stay outside the city."

Bearing Rama's sandals in his hands, with all reverence, Bharatha turned back. He established himself in a little village called Nandigram, on the outskirts of Ayodhya, installed Rama's sandals on the throne, and ruled the country as a regent.

4

ENCOUNTERS IN EXILE

After Bharatha's departure, Rama left Chitrakuta. Dwelling in the proximity of Ayodyha, he feared, might encourage people to come across the river and persuade him to return home. He felt that such encounters would dilute the value and purpose of his renunciation. He decided to move farther into the forests. Though Lakshmana had built at Chitrakuta a hut with mud, bamboo, palm leaves, wood, and other materials available in the forest, and decorated and brightened the floor and walls with coloured earth (so well designed and constructed that Rama was constrained to ask in admiration, "When did you learn to be such a fine house-builder?") Rama left this beautiful cottage and moved on. In the course of their journey, they came upon several sages residing in their ashrams, all of whom received Rama's party as honoured guests. Among these were Athri and his wife Anusuya, who gave all her jewellery and clothes to Sita, and compelled her to wear them then and there. Rama went on to Dandaka forest, and then on to Panchvati (on the advice of Sage Agasthya). On the way he noticed, perched on a rock, Jatayu, the Great Eagle. Jatayu explained to Rama that although he was now in the form of a bird his origin was divine. He proved to be possessed of extraordinary ripeness of spirit and wisdom. He had been a great friend of Dasaratha at one time, associated with him on battlefields; they had been so close that at one time Dasaratha had remarked, "You are the soul, I am the body. We are one."

Rama was happy to meet a contemporary of his father's in this remoteness. Jatayu also welcomed him as his foster parent. When he learnt of the death of Dasaratha, he broke down and swore to end his life. But Rama and Lakshmana pleaded, "Having lost our father, just when we found solace in meeting you, we cannot bear to hear of your ending your life. Please desist." In deference to their wish Jatayu promised to live at least until Rama could return to Ayodhya after his term of exile, meanwhile taking upon himself the task of protecting them, especially Sita, during their sojourn at Panchvati. He led the way to Panchvati on the banks of the Godavari, suggesting, "While I fly, follow me in the shadow of my wings."

When Rama, Lakshmana, and Sita reached the Godavari River's bank, they were enchanted with their surroundings. Rama felt a great tenderness for his wife, who looked particularly lovely adorned with the ornaments given by Anusuya. Rama glanced at her whenever a beautiful object caught his eye. Every tint of the sky, every shape of a flower or bud, every elegant form of a creeper reminded him of some aspect or other of Sita's person.

They reached Panchvati, set in sylvan surroundings in the proximity of the river. Lakshmana, adept as he had proved to be, had already gone ahead and created a home for them with clay, thatch, leaves, and wood, enclosed with a fence, and affording protection from sun and rain, and privacy for Rama and Sita. Again Rama was delighted with his brother's engineering and architectural genius, and entered his new home filled with a sense of wonder. For all its idyllic charm, and in the joy of companionship of Sita, Rama never lost sight of his main purpose in settling down in this region—he had come here to encounter and destroy the asuras, the fiends who infested this area, causing suffering and hardship to all the good souls who only wanted to be left alone to pursue their spiritual aims in peace. Rama's whole purpose of incarnation was ultimately to destroy Ravana, the chief of the asuras, abolish fear from the hearts of men and gods, and establish peace, gentleness, and justice in the world.

And so one evening, when he noticed in the woods, amidst the creepers and plants in his front yard, a damsel of the utmost beauty, he became wary. The damsel's anklets jingled at her feet

when she walked, her eyes flashed, her teeth sparkled, her fig-
ure, waist, and bosom were that of a chiselled figure. Rama,
even the austere Rama, was struck by her beauty. As she dallied
at his gate, he stood staring at her in wonderment, and when
she flashed her smile at him and approached him half-shyly,
Rama said, "Oh, perfect one, you are welcome. May you be
blessed. Tell me who you are, where you have come from, who
are your kinsmen, and what you are doing, so accomplished
and beautiful, in this solitude? What is the purpose of your visit
here?"

"Here I answer your question with humility. I am the daugh-
ter of Sage Visravas, son of Pulastya, who was Brahma's own
son; half-sister of that friend of Lord Shiva, Kubera, the wealth-
iest man and the most generous in all the worlds, who lives in
the north; and direct younger sister of one at whose name gods
in heaven and emperors of this world tremble, and who once
tried to lift Mount Kailas itself with Lord Shiva and Parvathi on
it. My name is Kamavalli."

Rama asked in surprise, "Do you mean that you are Ravana's
sister?"

"Yes, I am," she replied proudly.

He concealed the many misgivings that stirred in him and
asked, "If you are Ravana's sister, how have you come to pos-
sess this form?"

"I abhorred the ways of my brother and other relations and
their demoniac qualities; I abhor sin and cruelty and prize all
virtues and goodness; I want to be different from my kinsmen
and I have earned this personality through constant prayers."

"Oh, beauty, will you explain why, when you happen to be
the sister of that overlord of three worlds, Ravana, you have not
come surrounded with attendants and bearers, but all alone,
unescorted?"

She answered, "I have chosen to reject evil-doers such as my
brother and the rest and thrown my lot with those who are
saintly and good; and I shun the association of my own people,
that's the reason why I'm alone. I have come alone now—
mainly to see you. . . . I want help from you. Will you grant it?"

"Tell me your purpose. If it's right and proper, I'll consider it."

"It's not proper for a woman of breeding to state her inner-most feelings, but I dare to do it, driven to desperation by the attacks of the god of love. Forgive me . . ."

Rama understood her purpose. He realized that she had only an appearance of quality, and was really cheap and shameless. He remained silent. Whereupon, unable to decide whether he was encouraging or discouraging, she confirmed, "Not know-ing that you were here, I was wasting my youth and beauty in serving ascetics and sages. Now that I have found you, my womanhood can have its own fulfillment."

Rama felt a pity for her, and, not wanting to seem hostile, tried to argue her out of her purpose. Overcoming his revul-sion, he said, "I am of the warrior class, you are a brahmin, and I cannot marry you." She had an immediate answer for this.

"Oh, if that is your only objection to me, then my ebbing hopes are buoyed. Please know that my mother was of the asura class; and for a woman of that class, union with all castes is permissible."

Rama was still calm when he mentioned his second objec-tion: "I am a human, and you are of the rakshasa class; and I cannot marry you."

Undaunted, she replied, "I humbly remind you, as I have al-ready mentioned, that I have no mind to remain in our class, but am seeking the company of saints and sages; oh, you, who look like Vishnu himself, I should no longer be considered to belong to Ravana's family or to be his sister; I have already told you that. If that's all your objection, then I have hope."

Rama still felt kindly toward her, and said without irritation or acerbity, with a touch of lightheartedness, "After all, a bride of your class should be presented properly, when she happens to be a sister of men of eminence such as Kubera and Ravana. You should not be offering yourself like this in matrimony."

"When two persons meet and inwardly have attained union, there is no need for elders to take any formal part in such a marriage. It's sanctioned under Gandharva rites. Also, my broth-ers are hostile to ascetics, and stop at nothing when they want to fight them; they observe no rules or disciplines under those circumstances; you are alone and you wear the robes of ascetics, and if they see you, nothing can stop them from attacking you. But if they realize that we are married like Gandharvas, they will relent, be kind to you, and even adopt you and confer on you honours and wealth and overlordship of several worlds . . . think of it."

At this Rama was amused and remarked, "Ah, is this one way in which the fruits of my penance and sacrifices are to be realized—achieve the grace of rakshasas, gain domestic bliss through your company, and all the conquests thereof?" She noted his smile, but missed the irony and was about to say something else when she noted that there was another woman in the picture. Sita had just emerged from the cottage. At the sight of her, Kamavalli looked stunned. She scrutinized the vision inch by inch and was filled with the profoundest admiration as well as despair. If that beautiful creature was the occupant of the cottage, there was no hope for her. She demanded bluntly, "Who is this?" Sita's radiance seemed to precede her actual arrival. Kamavalli had first noticed the light and only then had she seen Sita engulfed in that effulgence. Her jaw fell at this spectacle; for a moment she lost herself in gazing on this pair whose beauty complemented each other; if there was anywhere in creation a male with the perfection of attributes, to be matched by a perfect female, here it was. Kamavalli momentarily forgot her own infatuation in the spell cast by the presence of this pair. But it was only a fleeting distraction. Her passion soon revived. She assumed that Sita too was one who had sneaked up to Rama on some forest path and attached herself to him. She could not be this man's wife, as no wife would care to face the hardship of a forest existence. He must surely have left his wife, if he had one, back at home, and now lived with this woman in the forest.

Kamavalli said to Rama very seriously, "Great one! Don't let this creature come near you. Don't be misled by her appearance, it's not her own, she has assumed it through black art. Actually she is a rakshasa woman; drive her off before she does you any harm. This forest is full of such deceivers."

She might well have been confessing this of herself—her own normal appearance being that of a demon with wild, matted hair, flame-coloured fang-like teeth, enormous stature, and a belly swollen with the meat and blood of animals she had gorged on in her never-ending gluttony. Her name was Soorpanaka. Her brother Ravana had assigned this Dandaka forest as her own domain, leaving her free to live here as she pleased, assisted by a number of ruthless demons led by Kara—the fiercest devil ever conceived. Here she held her court and ravaged the forests. In the course of her wanderings, she saw Rama and fell in love and decided to seduce him by every art in her power. As a first step, through certain incantations, she transformed herself into a comely maiden. Now, when she warned Rama of Sita's true nature as she imagined it, he began to laugh and remarked, "Ah, how true! No one can deceive you, being yourself so transparent! Your piercing perception is truly admirable; nothing can escape your eyes. Look well now at this sorceress at my side, so that she may realize who she is."

Taking him at his word, Soorpanaka glared at Sita fiercely and shouted, "Get out! Who are you? You have no business to disturb us, when I'm engaged in a private talk with my lover. Be gone!" In her anger, her real tone and personality came through unconcealed. At the sight of it, Sita shook with fright and ran to Rama's arms and clung to him. This further enraged Soorpanaka, who moved towards her with a menacing gesture.

Rama felt it was time to end her visit. Even a moment of jesting with an asura is likely to lead to incalculable evil consequences. So he said, "Do nothing that will bring on retribution and suffering. Please be gone before my brother Lakshmana notices you. He will be angry. Please go away quickly before he comes."

"All the gods in heaven, Brahma, Vishnu, and Shiva, Indra and the god of love, Manmatha himself, seek me and pray for my favours and attention. I'm unattainable and rare, as they all know. When this is the case, how can you talk so contemptuously to me, and go on desiring and trusting this treacherous sorceress at your side? Explain your inconsiderate and thoughtless attitude."

Rama felt that any further conversation with her would prove useless. Obstinate and unmoving, she built her edifice of falsehoods higher and higher; so he turned and, holding Sita close to him, walked back calmly and gracefully into his ashram.

When the door was shut in her face, Soorpanaka felt so distraught that she almost swooned. Recovering, she reflected, "He has spurned me in no uncertain terms and turned his back on me; he is completely infatuated with that woman." Finding that there was nothing more for her to do there, she withdrew to her own lair beyond the woods and went to bed. She was shrivelling in the heat of passion. As it had once been for Sita, the same love-sickness proved a great torment to this monstrous woman too. Everything irritated her and aggravated her agony. When the moonlight flooded the earth, she roared at the moon and wished she could set the serpent Rahu to swallow it; when the cool breeze touched her, she howled imprecations at it, and rose as if determined to destroy the god of love himself, whose shafts were piercing her heart. Unable to stand the pain inflicted by her present surroundings, she entered a mountain cave infested with deadly serpents and shut herself in it. There she was the victim of hallucinations. Rama in his full form seemed to stand before her again and again, and she fancied she embraced him and fondled his broad shoulders and chest. When the illusion passed, she cried, "Why do you torment me in this way? Why do you refuse to unite with me, and quench the fire that's burning me?" After the turmoil of the night, sheer exhaustion found her calmer when morning came. She decided on her strategy. "If I cannot attain him, I will not live any more. But I'll make one more attempt. He does not care for me because of the spell cast by that woman. If I remove her from his side and put her away, he will then naturally take to me." This gave her a fresh energy.

Daylight in some measure lessened the pangs of love, and she came out of her cave. She went along to Panchvati and prowled around, looking for a chance. She saw Rama come out of his hut and proceed towards the banks of the Godavari for his morning bath and prayers. "Now is the time," she said to herself. "If I miss it, I'll lose him for ever. It's a matter of life and death for me. After all, when he finds her gone, he'll begin to accept me." Though the sight of Rama had sent a tremor

through her body, she restrained herself from falling at his feet
and confessing her love. She watched him go, and presently Sita
emerged from the hut to gather flowers. "This chance is not to
be missed," Soorpanaka told herself. Every decision seemed to
her a valuable step in her pursuit of Rama. She began to stalk
behind Sita cunningly like an animal following its prey. She
would pounce and grab and put her away, and when Rama
came back, he'd find her in Sita's place. Excellent plan as far as
the idea went, but she did not reckon there could be another
outcome to it. In her concentration on the beloved image of
Rama, and on the movements of Sita, she failed to notice that
she was being watched. Lakshmana had posted himself, as nor-
mally he did, on an eminence shaded with trees, and was watch-
ing in all directions. When he saw Soorpanaka near the hut, he
became alert; when he found her stalking Sita, he sprang down
on her. She had just laid hands on Sita, when she found herself
grabbed, held down by her hair, and kicked in the stomach.

"Oh! a woman!" Lakshmana muttered, and decided to spare
her life. Instead of taking out his arrow, he pulled out his sword
and chopped off her nose, ears, and breasts. When his anger
subsided, he let go her hair.

When Rama returned home from the river, she was mutilated
and bloody and screaming her life out. Lamenting to the skies,
she called upon her powerful brothers, reciting their valour in
all the worlds; repeating again and again how impossible that
the sister of such eminent personages should have to suffer this
mutilation and humiliation in the hands of two ordinary human
beings, dressed as ascetics but carrying arms and attacking peo-
ple treacherously. To think that human creatures, which served
as food for her poor relations, should have dared to do this to
Ravana's sister! . . .

Rama did not ask, "What has happened?" but "Who are you
in such a bloody state? Where do you come from?"

She replied, "Don't you know me? Why do you pretend? We
met last evening and you were so attentive to me! Ah!" she
cried, her infatuation reviving.

Rama understood. "You are the same one, are you?" he asked.
He made no other comment.

She replied, amidst her agony, "You don't find me beautiful? No wonder! If one's nose and ears and breasts are lopped off, will not one's beauty suffer?"

Rama turned to Lakshmana and asked, "What did she do?"

Lakshmana answered, "With fire in her eyes, she was about to fall on Janaki,* and I prevented it."

Soorpanaka now explained, "Naturally, it's just and right that I hate anyone who has deprived me of my beloved's company." In her mind she had treated Rama as her own property. "Would it not inflame a woman's heart to see her beloved taken away?"

Rama said simply, "Go away before your tongue utters worse words, which may bring you more harm. Go back to your own people."

Soorpanaka made one last attempt to gain Rama's love. She said, "Even now it's not too late. My brother Ravana will pardon you for what you have done if he knows we are married; he will also make you the overlord of several worlds, placed above all the gods. It's not too late. On the other hand, if anyone comments on my nose or ears, he will wipe them out. So, do not hesitate. No one will dare to say that I have no nose or ears or breasts. I've still eyes, which can feast on your broad chest and shoulders, and my arms are intact to embrace you. I love you madly. I'll be your slave and make all rakshasas your slaves. I can't survive without you. Have pity on me. I'll do anything you command." She was rolling in the dust with blood gushing, but nothing lessened her ardour. She continued, "My kinsmen are ruthless, and will be reckless when they find that I have been injured like this—they will destroy blindly, everything, including you. They will wipe out mankind. But if you take me, I can intercede on your behalf, and they will spare you and all your people. . . . You'll be the cause of either the destruction of mankind or its survival."

"The longer I let you speak, the worse things you say. Now go to your own people, and bring back with you all those powerful men and more. I can meet them, one by one as they come or all together. I can deal with them. Now begone. Understand

*Another name for Sita.

now, my mission in life is to root out the rakshasas from the face of this earth, and till I achieve it, I'll be here."

Even after suffering mutilation at the hands of Lakshmana, Soorpanaka stood there and persisted in appealing to Rama to accept her, hinting that through her magical powers she could appear beautiful again. At this point Rama felt that he ought to explain to her who he was, and how he had come to be here with his wife and brother. Further, he made it plain again that his mission in life would be to wipe out the asura class. He recounted how he had destroyed Thataka and her brood.

Far from discouraging her, this actually gave Soorpanaka another idea. "If that's your purpose, you know, I could be your best ally—if you do not spurn me for my appearance, if you do not reject me for my enormous teeth and large mouth. If you marry me, I will teach you all the arts and tricks, magical and others, that make my people superb and invincible. I can teach you how to defeat them, but you must treat me kindly. You must accept me. . . . Even if you cannot give up your slender companion—well, don't view me as an impossible addition. Would I be one too many? No. I'll help you by revealing to you all the tricks and trickeries of your enemies, so that you may attain complete victory over them. 'A serpent's feet are known to another serpent.' Even if your mind does not allow you to give up your wife . . . take me as a third partner, in your fight against the rakshasas, when my brother, who once kept the sun and the moon in captivity—and I'm not his inferior in valour—when he is defeated and gone, then at least let your brother Lakshmana marry me; and let me be with you when you return in triumph to Ayodhya. When we return, do not be worried that a person without a nose is accompanying you; please understand that I can create any shape for myself. If by chance, Lakshmana ever questions, "How can I live with a woman without a nose," tell him that he can in the same way as you live with one who is without any waist."*

---

*A subtle compliment to Sita's figure; a slender waist being an aesthetic point stressed often and in various ways by classical poets.

When she said this, Lakshmana was so enraged that he declared, "Brother, have I your permission to put an end to her? Otherwise she will never leave us alone!" Rama thought it over and said, "I think so too—if she persists and will not leave, that may be the only way." On hearing this, Soorpanaka picked herself up and left in haste. "Fools, do you think I meant what I said? Even after the loss of my features, I have stayed and spoken to you, only to understand the depth of your base mentality. I'll go but come back soon enough, with one who will be your Yama, a being more powerful than the elements, of the name of Kara"—and she left.

Kara, one of Ravana's stepbrothers, a dreaded warrior-demon with fourteen chiefs under him commanding an army, protected Soorpanaka and carried out her orders. After leaving Panchvati, Soorpanaka stormed in at his court, displayed her injuries, and cried, "Two human beings who have moved into our realm have done this to me."

"Two human beings!"

"Ah, wonderful sons of Dasaratha, so sagelike in appearance, but armed for the purpose of exterminating our clan. They have with them a woman of unearthly beauty; when I tried to seize her, these two humans fell on me and hacked me thus."

Kara looked closely at the damage done to her and thundered, "Death to those two. Not only they, but all human beings shall be stamped out." He sprang up to go into action. Fourteen commanders at once surrounded him and said, "Does it mean that you have no confidence in us that you should start out this way yourself? Leave this task to us. We will go and settle it."

Kara agreed. "So be it. You are right. If I wage war on these tiny petty creatures, the gods will mock us. Go and feast on their blood, but bring back the woman carefully."

Carrying a variety of arms such as spears and tridents and scimitars and hatchets, the commanders, led by Soorpanaka, marched on towards Rama's cottage. Soorpanaka stopped at a distance and pointed Rama out to them. "There he is, mark him." The fourteen asuras muttered, "Shall we bind and take him, or toss him in the air and kill him, or use the piercing lance on him?"

Soorpanaka said, "Bring that man alive. I will deal with him."

When he saw them approaching, Rama ordered Lakshmana, "Guard Sita. Don't leave her side." He took out his bow, slung his sword into position, girt himself for the fight, and emerged from his cottage with the anger of a lion. The battle began and ended quickly. Rama's arrows knocked down the weapons the asuras bore and severed their heads. Soorpanaka fled from the field and reported to Kara the disaster that had befallen her chiefs.

Kara sounded his tocsin and gathered an army of powerful rakshasas; they made their way to Panchvati and surrounded Rama's ashram without any doubt that they would end the career of the two foolhardy human beings. They had plans to surround the cottage, fall on it at a given moment, and wipe out the landmark with its occupants. With shouts and screams calculated to shake the nerves of their victims, they flourished their weapons and converged on the cottage. This phase of the battle was a little more prolonged but the result was the same as before.

Rama defeated Kara and his allies. Soorpanaka watched from afar, understood the trend of events, snatched a brief moment to approach and cry over the mangled corpses strewn around, including that of her champion and brother Kara, and decided it was time for her to leave the area. She fled to Lanka to convey the news of the disaster to her brother Ravana.

5

THE GRAND TORMENTOR

Ravana, the supreme lord of this and other worlds, sat in his durbar hall, surrounded by a vast throng of courtiers and attendants. The kings of this earth whom he had reduced to vassaldom stood about with their hands upraised in an attitude of perpetual salutation, lest at any moment Ravana should turn in their direction and think that they were not sufficiently servile. Beauties gathered from all the worlds surrounded him, singing, dancing, ministering to his wants, ever ready to give him pleasure and service, with all their eyes fixed on him watching for the slightest sign of command. Every minute vast quantities of flowers were rained on him by his admirers. He had also enslaved the reigning gods and put them to perform menial tasks in his court. Among them Vayu, the god of wind, was there to blow away faded flowers and garlands, and generally sweep the hall clean. Yama, the god of death, was employed to sound the gong each hour to tell the time of day. The god of fire was in charge of all illumination and kept lamps, incense, and camphor flames alit. The Kalpataru, the magic tree that yielded any wish, taken away from Indra, was also there to serve Ravana. Sage Narada sat there gently playing his veena. The gurus—Brihaspathi, who guided the gods, and Sukracharya, who guided the asuras—men possessing the finest intellects, were also there ready to advise Ravana when asked and to act generally as soothsayers.

Into this setting crashed Soorpanaka, screaming so loudly that all the men, women, and children of the city came rushing out of their homes and crowded the northern portal of the palace, where Soorpanaka had made her entry. She dashed up and fell before Ravana's throne, crying, "See what has happened to me!"

When Ravana observed her state, he thundered, "What is the meaning of this? Who has done it?"—in such a tone that all nature shrank and slunk away from the scene. Gods held their breath unable to gauge the upheaval that would follow when Ravana struck in revenge. While everyone in the assembly held his breath and waited, Ravana inquired with deliberate calmness, "Who has done this to you?"

Soorpanaka explained in detail and concluded, referring to Rama, "Even if I had a thousand tongues, I could never fully explain his beauty and the grandeur of his personality. Even if one had a thousand eyes one could not take in the splendour of this being. His strength is unmatched. Single-handed he wiped out all our army." She realized that she had made a blunder revealing too much of her inner feelings for Rama and corrected herself by adding, "For all his looks, what a cruel heart he has! His mission in life is to wipe out our whole family, clan, class from the face of this earth."

"Ah," cried Ravana, challenged. "We will see about that. But tell me why he did this to you. How did you provoke him?"

"He has a woman who should be yours. If you win her I fear all your present favourites will be thrown out. I also fear that you will surrender to her all your powers, valour, possessions, and conquests and make yourself her abject devotee. Her name is Sita. I was so overcome by her beauty that I waited and watched for a chance and attempted to snatch her and bring her to you as a present."

Ravana's interest shifted from revenge to love and he said, "Why didn't you?"

"When I seized her, this man's brother—Ah! how strong he was!—fell on me and slashed my face."

"Tell me all about her. . . ." Ravana commanded, ignoring all other issues.

Soorpanaka described Sita from head to toe in minute detail. The picture she conjured up was convincing and Ravana fell madly in love with her image. He became restless and unhappy. Every syllable that Soorpanaka uttered gave him both pleasure and pain. Soorpanaka urged him to set forth and capture Sita. Finally she said, "When you have succeeded in getting that woman, keep her for yourself; but be sure to surrender the man Rama to my hands. I'll deal with him." She had no doubt that her strategy to separate Sita from Rama was going to succeed and then Rama would naturally turn to her for love.

Ravana felt uneasy. He rose abruptly and left the hall, unwilling to let the assembly notice his state of mind. They rained flowers on him and uttered blessings and recited his glory as usual when he strode down the passage. His ten heads were held erect and his eyes looked straight ahead, not noticing the people standing about in respectful array; his mind was seething with ideas for the conquest of Sita. Soorpanaka's words had lit an all-consuming flame within him. He ignored his wives, who were awaiting his favours, and passed on to his own private chamber, where he shut the door and flung himself on his luxurious bed. He lay there tossing, unable to rid his mind of the figure conjured up by Soorpanaka's words. It was a total obsession; he felt tormented and raged against his surroundings, which appeared to aggravate his suffering. Presently he realized that his bed and the chamber were uninhabitable. The place seemed to be scorching hot. He got up and moved out unceremoniously to the woods, leaving his attendants and aides wondering what kind of seizure was driving him hither and thither. He moved to his garden house of pure marble and gold set amidst towering palmyra and flowering trees, and lay down on a pure white satin bed. When they saw him arrive, cuckoos and parrots in the trees silenced themselves.

The late winter with its light mist and cool wind proved uncomfortable to Ravana, who shouted at it the question, "What wretched season are you?"—whereupon the weather changed to early summer, a rather unwilling summer ushered in prematurely. One who found the wintry day too warm naturally found even the spring unbearable. Ravana cried out, "I do not want this weather. Let the monsoons come immediately."

The weather changed to suit his mood. On his order came the monsoon season with its cloud and damp air, but even that proved too warm for him. He shouted, "What kind of weather is this? You have brought back only the late winter, which was horrible."

His aides answered meekly, "Would we dare to disobey you? What we called down was really early rains, as your Lordship commanded."

Whereupon Ravana said, "Banish all seasons. Let them all get out of this world." As a consequence, there was a complete standstill in time. Minute, hour, day, month, and year lost their boundaries. And mankind was lost in a seasonless confusion. In spite of all this, there was no peace for Ravana. He was still scorched by a hopeless love for Sita.

When all measures for cooling himself had failed—such as covering his body with sandalwood paste and layers of tender leaves of a rare plant treated with essence of saffron—Ravana, who felt himself shrivelling in stature, said to those around him, "The moon is supposed to have cool moisture. Bring the moon down."

His messengers approached the moon, who normally avoided passage over Ravana's territory, and said, "Our King summons you. Don't be afraid. Come with us." The moon rose in full glory over the sea and timidly approached Ravana, bathing his surroundings in soft light.

But now Ravana asked his servants, "What made you bring the sun?" They answered, "The sun dare not come unasked nor would we dare to bring him here." When Ravana recognized the moon as the moon, he swore at him, "You are worthless, pale-faced, constantly worn out and trying to regain your shape again. You have no stamina or quality. You are contemptible. Is it possible that you are also stricken with thoughts of Sita? Take care if you ever entertain any ideas about that woman. Get out now, I don't want you here." He then ordered, "Let the night go. Get back daylight and the sun."

When the night suddenly ceased, all the people of the world were suddenly thrown into confusion. Lovers in bed found themselves suddenly exposed by daylight; those in a state of intoxication with wine were bewildered and embarrassed. Birds stirred in their nests not knowing what had happened. Lamps fed with oil and lit for a whole night faded in daylight. Astronomers who calculate the movement of the stars and planets and declare their positions through the almanacs were caught literally napping as they did not know day had come. Even the roosters remained silent, unable to adjust themselves to the sudden daylight. "Is this the sun? You call him the sun! He is once again the moon who was here a while ago and made my blood boil. This one is no better. Same as before. Don't lie," said Ravana. His servants assured him again that this was really the sun. Then he ordered the sun to go out and the crescent moon to rise; then the sea waves to remain silent; and then ordered total darkness to envelop the earth, causing confusion and suffering to its inhabitants. In that utter darkness Ravana suffered hallucinations of Sita's figure approaching and receding, and addressed it endearingly.

He had never seen anyone so beautiful in all the worlds where he had roamed at will. Still doubting his own vision, he ordered, "Fetch my sister at once." No time could be lost between his command and the execution thereof. Soorpanaka arrived. He asked her, "I see this woman before me. Is this the one you meant?"

Soorpanaka looked hard and said, "Oh, no. The person who stands before us is not a woman at all. It's Rama, that—that man. I don't see Sita here. You are only imagining. . . ."

"If it's mere imagination on my part, how is it you see Rama here?"

Soorpanaka merely said, "Ever since the day he did this damage to me, I find it impossible to forget him," trying not to be too explicit about her feelings for Rama, equivocating her meaning.

Ravana said, "Be that as it may, I am melting and dying for Sita. How shall I be saved now?"

Soorpanaka said, "You are the overlord of seven worlds, mightier than the mightiest. Why do you feel sad and unhappy? Go and get her; that is all. Take her. She is yours. Is there anything beyond your reach? Stir yourself. Leave this desolate mood. Go forth, snatch her, because she is yours, created for you and waiting for you." Thus she infused a new spirit in Ravana, and it made her secretly happy that her plan to get Sita out of the way was working out satisfactorily. She left.

Ravana felt reassured now and braced himself to take practical steps to achieve his aim. He sent out his servants to summon his advisers and minister immediately. With the least delay they began to arrive at Ravana's retreat by horseback, elephant, and chariots, and the gods in Heaven watched the traffic apprehensively, speculating as to what this sudden activity might bode for the universe. Ravana's consultations with the advisers were brief, being in the nature of an announcement to them of decisions already made. Somehow he valued the formality of being counselled. He then summoned his chariot, got into it alone, and flew towards a retreat where his uncle, Mareecha, was meditating in a cave. Mareecha had made two attempts to attack Rama and both had failed. The first had been the one at Sidhasrama, to avenge his mother Thataka's death, when Rama's arrow had flung him far out into the sea. Later he had made another attempt, failed to kill Rama, and retreated into the woods, forswearing a career of violence.

Now, at the sight of Ravana, Mareecha felt uneasy, but received him courteously and inquired, "What can I do for you?"

Ravana said, "My mind is shattered. I am going through a phase of utter shame. The gods doubtless watch and rejoice, but on our supreme race a great shame has fallen and we have to hang our heads down and crawl aside like faceless worms. A human creature has stationed himself in Dandaka and has dared to challenge our supremacy. He has mutilated my dear sister's face. Your beloved niece is now without nose, ears, or breasts. He chopped them off when she approached his miserable hut."

Mareecha already had an inkling as to who the human creature was, and when he heard the sound, "Rama," he immediately said, "Keep away from him." Ravana felt irritated and declared, "I won't. Are you suggesting that we should tremble before him?"

"Let us not go near him."

Ravana said, "Very well, I'll not go near him, but only snatch away his woman and keep her with me. For after all I do not wish to engage myself in a fight with a mere human being. But he must be taught a lesson for his presumptuousness and reckless arrogance. One sure way of hurting a human being is to deprive him of his female companion."

Mareecha, who was now putting forth his best effort to live a new life and practise all the moral and spiritual values, cried, "It's immoral. Coveting another's wife. . . ."

"She had no business to become his wife. She should have met me first," said Ravana, his first phase of forlorn depression now giving place to levity.

Mareecha's present outlook did not permit him to accept Ravana's proposals passively. He cried, "You have the grace of Shiva on you. You are endowed with eminence and power. Do not cheapen yourself with such adventures. You should not become a subject of gossip in this or other worlds."

"So you want me to watch indifferently when my sister is hurt and humiliated! I don't need your advice. I only want your help."

"In what manner?" asked Mareecha, feeling that he was nearing the end of his spiritual attempts and perhaps the end of his life too.

"I have a plan to take that woman away and you have a part in it."

Mareecha said, "A sort of drum-beat goes on within my mind, sounding and re-sounding the message that you are seeking your own destruction and the liquidation of our race."

"How dare you belittle my own power and exalt that creature who has not spared my sister!" Ravana asked angrily. "If I show patience now, it's because I still treat you as my uncle." And Mareecha retorted, "It's on the same basis of relationship that I wish you to save yourself from annihilation."

"You forget that I once shook Shiva's abode, the Kailas mountain itself. My strength is unlimited."

"But Rama is the one who broke in two Shiva's bow, which was as big as the Meru Mountain."

"You are still praising him," Ravana said grimly.

"It's because I watched him destroy my mother and brother Subahu. I saw Viswamithra impart to him all the powers in his command and thus Rama now possesses asthras immeasurable in power and numbers and he can face any encounter with assurance."

"Enough of your rhapsody. I will split you with my sword, if you persist, and then achieve my end without your help, that's all." Mareecha suppressed his judgement and said, "I only thought of your welfare, which is my chief concern. I want you to live long and be happy."

This pleased Ravana, who put his arm on Mareecha's shoulder and said, "You are good and strong and your shoulders are broad and high like hillocks. Now go and fetch that Sita. Hurry up. And as to your prophecy, if I have to die for it, let it be Rama's arrow that pierces my heart rather than the insidious, minute ones from the bow of the god of love."

"Tell me what I should do. What is left for me to do? The time when I decided to avenge the death of my mother and brother, two companions and I approached Rama in the shape of spotted deer. Rama killed the other two with a single arrow and I barely escaped with my life. Then I adopted a new philosophy. Now again, what is there left for me to do?" reflected Mareecha woefully, concluding that he would rather be killed by Rama than by his own nephew, who had just threatened him.

Ravana merely said, "You will have to grab her by some trickery."

"It would be nobler and more befitting for one of your status," Mareecha replied, "to fight Rama on this issue and take Sita as a prize of your conquest."

"Do you want me to employ an army to tackle that mortal? I can put an end to his nuisance once for all, but I do not wish to take that step, as the woman may immolate herself if she finds her man dead, and our whole plan would be ruined."

Mareecha realized that his strategy to end Ravana's career would not work. There was no escape for him. Resigning himself to his fate, he said, "Tell me what to do."

Seizing the idea from Mareecha's own narration, Ravana firmly suggested, without leaving him any choice, "Assume the form of a golden deer, and draw her out. I'll do the rest . . . It's the only way to get at her without hurting anyone."

Mareecha agreed. "Yes, I'll go this moment and carry out your wishes." But he was fully aware of the consequences that would befall him immediately and Ravana later. Mareecha went forth, gloomily reflecting, "Twice have I escaped Rama's arrow; now, this third time, I shall be doomed. I am like a fish in a poisoned pond. Sooner or later I am bound to die, whether I stay in it or get out of it."

Mareecha went to Dandaka forest. In the vicinity of Panchvati, he assumed the form of a golden deer and strutted before Rama's cottage. Attracted by its brilliance, other deer came up and surrounded the golden deer. Sita, strolling in her garden, noticed it, hurried back into the cottage, and requested of Rama, "There is an animal at our gate with a body of shining gold, and its legs are set with precious stones. It's a dazzling creature. Please catch it for me."

The fates were at work and this was to be a crucial moment in their lives. Normally, Rama would have questioned Sita's fancy, but today he blindly accepted her demand and said cheerfully, "Yes, of course you shall have it. Where is it?" and he rose to go out.

At this point Lakshmana interceded. "I would not go near it. It may be just an illusion presented before us. It's not safe. Who has ever heard of an animal made of gold and gems? It's a trick, if ever there was one."

Rama replied, "Brahma's creations are vast and varied. No one can say that he knows all the creatures of this earth. How can you assert that there can be no such creature of splendour?"

Sita interposed impatiently, "While you are debating, the animal will be gone. Please come out and see it for yourself."

Rama came out of the cottage, saw it, and said, "It's a wonderful creature. Stay here. I will get it for you."

Sita said, "I'll keep it with me as my pet and take it back to Ayodhya when our exile ends."

Lakshmana once again tried to prevent this pursuit. But Rama brushed aside his argument. "It's harmless to pursue it. If it is some infernal creature in this form, it will reveal itself when it is shot at. If it is not, we will take it intact and Sita will have a plaything. Either way we cannot ignore it."

"We can't go after it when we do not know who has set it before us. If it's harmless, it would be wrong to hunt it. In any case, it is best to keep away from it." When he found Rama obstinate, Lakshmana said, "Please stay here. I will go after it and try to find out the truth of it."

Sita became insistent and said sullenly, "You will never get it, I know," and turned round and went back into the hermitage, annoyed and irritated.

Rama felt sad that there should be such an argument over an innocent wish of his wife, who had ungrudgingly thrown her lot with his. He said to Lakshmana, "Let me go and catch it myself. Meanwhile, guard her." With his bow held ready, he approached the golden deer. His mind did not admit Lakshmana's words of caution; it went on echoing Sita's plaintive appeal and he resolved to himself, "She shall have it, and then she will surely smile again." The chase began. The deer waited for his approach and darted off again and again. In the mood of the chase, Rama had not noticed how far he had been drawn out or how long it had lasted. Forest paths, mountain tracks, and valleys he had traversed trying to keep pace with the elusive deer. A blind determination, a challenge, and behind them a desire to please his wife—all these drew him on as the splendorous animal receded farther and farther.

Suddenly it dawned on him that he was being duped. Lakshmana was right after all. He ought not to have so blindly obeyed his wife. Automatically his hand took out an arrow and shot it at the animal, just as Mareecha, guessing Rama's thoughts, made a desperate attempt to escape. But it was too late. Rama's arrow as ever reached its target. Mareecha screamed, "Oh, Lakshmana! Oh, Sita! help me . . ." assuming the voice of Rama.

After disposing of Mareecha in this manner, Rama turned back, rather worried that Mareecha's cry might have been heard by Sita. "Lakshmana will help her to guess what has happened," he thought, for he admired Lakshmana's sagacity and understanding; but realizing that he had been drawn quite far away from Panchvati, he hurried back towards his cottage.

Sita, hearing the cry of Mareecha, said to Lakshmana, "Something has happened to my lord. Go and help him."

"No harm can befall Rama. Be assured of it. One who has vanquished all the demons in this world will not be harmed by a mere animal, if indeed, as you think, it is an animal. It was an asura, now finished off, and the cry was false and assumed, aimed precisely at you."

"This is no time for explanations or speculation," she said. As she was talking the cry was heard a second time. "Oh, Lakshmana! Oh, Sita!" And Sita was seized with panic and lost control of herself completely. She cried, "Do not stand there and talk! Go, go and save Rama!"

"He is the saviour and needs no help from others, my respected sister-in-law. Wait, be patient for a while, and you will see him before you, and then you will laugh at your own fears."

Sita had no ear for any explanation and went on repeating, "Go, go and save him! How can you stay here talking! I'm surprised at your calmness." As Lakshmana kept on asking her to remain calm, she became more and more worked up and began to talk wildly. "You who have never left his side since your birth, who followed him into the forest—at a moment like this, instead of rushing to his side, you stand there chattering away at me. This looks very very strange to me!"

Once again Lakshmana tried to set her mind at rest. "You have apparently not understood the nature of Rama. There is no power which can reduce him to cry for help. If Rama was really threatened, the whole universe and all creation would have trembled and collapsed by now, for he is no ordinary mortal. . . ."

Sita's eyes flashed anger and sorrow. "It's improper for you to stay here with me and talk coldly this way. Strange! Strange! Anyone who has been close to my lord for even a brief moment ought to be prepared to lay down his life for him. Yet you, who were born and bred with him and attached yourself to him through everything—you stand here unmoved and unaffected by his cry for help. If you don't want to save him, there is nothing more I can do, nor anyone I could turn to for support. The only thing left will be for me to build a fire and throw myself into it. . . ."

Sita's insinuations and lack of trust in him pained Lakshmana deeply. He pondered over her words and said, "No need for you to harm yourself. Only I shudder at the import of your words. I'll obey you now. Do not be anxious. This very second I'll leave. I only hesitated because your order goes against the command of my brother. I'll go, and may the gods protect you from harm!"

"If I don't go, she will kill herself," he reasoned. "If I go, she will be in danger. I'd rather be dead than facing such a dilemma. . . . I'll go, and what is destined will happen. Dharma alone should protect her." He said to Sita, "Our elder Jatayu is there to watch us, and he will guard you."

The moment Lakshmana left, Ravana, who had been watching, emerged from his hiding place. He stood at the gate of Panchvati cottage and called, "Who is there? Anyone inside to welcome a *sanyasi*?" He was in the garb of a hermit, lean, scraggy, and carrying a staff and a wooden begging bowl in his hand. His voice shook as if with old age, his legs trembled, as he called again, "Is there anyone living in this hut?"

Sita opened the door and saw the old man and said, "You are welcome, sir. What do you want?"

Ravana was overwhelmed by the vision before him. Sita invited him in and gave him a seat while his mind buzzed with a thousand thoughts. "She should be mine. I'll make her the queen of my empire and spend the rest of my days in obeying her command and pleasing her in a million ways. I'll do nothing else in life except enjoy her company. . . . Ah! how perceptive and helpful my sister has been! Not a word of exaggeration in her description. Absolutely perfect. Perfection . . . How good of my darling sister to have thought of me when she saw this angel! I shall reward my sister by making her the queen of my empire. She shall rule in my place, while I live in the paradise of this woman's company." He had already forgotten that he had intended to make Sita the queen of his empire.

While his mind was busy with these pleasant plans, Sita was inquiring, "How do you come to be found on this lonely forest path—at your age? Where do you come from?"

He woke up from his day-dreaming to answer, "Well, there is one . . ." and proceeded to give a detailed account of himself in the third person—as the mightiest in creation, favourite of the great Lord Shiva himself, powerful enough to order the sun and the moon to move in or out of their orbits as he pleased. "All the gods wait upon him to do his slightest bidding, all the divine damsels, Urvasi, Thilothama and the others, are ever ready to massage his feet and strap his sandals on. He is greater than Indra; his capital is unmatched, a magnificent city; he commands all the power, wealth, and glories of this world. Thousands of women wait anxiously for his favour, but he is waiting and looking for the most perfect beauty in creation. He is learned, just, handsome, in vigour and youthfulness unmatched. I have stayed in the glory of his presence for a long time and am now returning home this way."

"Why should a saintly one like you have chosen to live in that rakshasa country, leaving cities where good men are to be found and the forest where sages live?"

"They are good people, not harmful or cruel like the so-called gods. The rakshasa clan have been misrepresented and misunderstood. They are kind and enlightened and particularly good to *sadhus* like me."

"Those who live amidst asuras could easily become asuras too," Sita remarked naïvely.

Ravana said, "Asuras can be good to those who are good to them. Since they are the most powerful in all the worlds, what could be wiser than to live in harmony with them?"

"But their days are numbered," said Sita. "My lord's mission in life is to rid this world of them and establish peace on earth."

"No human being can ever dare try it. It's like a little rabbit hoping to destroy an elephant herd."

"But have you not heard how my lord has vanquished Kara, Dushana, Virada, and the rest, single-handed?"

"Kara, Virada, and the rest were weaklings possessing neither bows nor armour—not a great task conquering them. Wait until you see, as you soon will, what happens to him when he has to meet the mighty Ravana, who has twenty shoulders!"

"What if he has twenty shoulders? Did not just a two-shouldered man like Parasurama once imprison Ravana till he cried for mercy?"

This statement enraged Ravana; his eyes became bloodshot with anger and he ground his teeth. Gradually he was losing his saintly disguise. Noticing the transformation, Sita began to feel puzzled and presently he loomed over her fearsomely in his natural form. Sita had no courage to utter any word.

Ravana said, "For your stupid statement, I would have crushed and eaten you, except for the fact you are a woman and I want you and will die if I don't have you. Oh, swanlike one, my ten heads have never bowed to any god in any world. But I will take off my crowns and touch your feet with my brow. Only be my queen and command me what to do."

Sita covered her ears with her hands. "How dare you speak thus! I am not afraid to lose my life, but if you wish to save yours, run and hide before Rama sees you."

"Rama's arrows cannot touch me; you could as well expect a mountain to split at the touch of a straw," Ravana said. "Be kind to me. I am dying for your love. I will give you a position greater than anything a goddess can have. Have consideration. Have mercy. I prostrate myself before you."

When Ravana fell to the floor, Sita recoiled and started weeping aloud, "O my lord! O, brother Lakshmana, come and help me."

At this Ravana, remembering an ancient curse that if he touched any woman without her consent, he would die that instant, dug the ground under Sita's feet, lifted it off with her, placed it in his chariot, and sped away.

Sita fainted, revived, desperately tried to jump off the chariot, cried, lamented, called upon the trees, birds, and animals and the fairies of the woods to bear witness and report her plight to Rama, and finally cursed Ravana as a coward and a trickster, who had adopted treacherous means only because he was afraid of Rama; otherwise would he not have faced Rama and fought him? Ravana only treated her words as a great joke and laughed at her. "You think too highly of Rama, but I don't. I do not care to fight him because it's beneath our dignity to confront a mere human being."

"Ah, yes, your class are ashamed to contend with humans, but you may covet and treacherously attack a helpless woman.

This is a noble achievement, I suppose! Stony-hearted rakshasas like you do not know what is wrong and what is right. If you have the courage to face my husband, stop your chariot immediately; don't drive it farther."

All this only amused Ravana, who laughed and bantered and uttered reckless pleasantries. At this moment, he felt an obstruction in the course of his flight. Jatayu, the great eagle who had promised to guard the children of his old colleague and friend Dasaratha, noticing the danger that had befallen Sita, shouted a challenge and obstructed Ravana's passage, hurling himself on Ravana with all his might. It was as if a mountain were hitting the speeding chariot. Before starting the actual battle, Jatayu appealed to Ravana to retrace his steps and take Sita back to Panchvati. He said, "You don't even have to go back; just stop and put her down, and I'll lead her back safely to her husband and you may run away before Rama comes."

Ravana laughed at this proposal. "Keep out of my way, you senile bird, go away."

Jatayu advised him, "Don't seek your own ruin, and the ruin of your whole clan, class, tribe, and all. Rama's arrows will end your career, have no doubt about it."

"Stop chattering away like this," Ravana commanded. "Let all those heroes you talk about come, bring them all, and I will deal with them. Whatever may happen, I'll not yield this treasure that I have acquired. . . . She will go with me."

Sita grew desperate and burst into tears. Jatayu said, "Don't fear. No harm will come to you. This demon will be destroyed by me. You don't have to worry about it at all"—and began his attack. The flapping of his enormous wings created the power of a storm, which shook and paralysed both Ravana and his chariot; then he hit and tore with his whole body, beak, and claws, with such force that Ravana's ensign with the symbol of a veena* was torn and the flagstaff was in fragments, his crowns were knocked off and fell to the ground, his royal canopy was in tatters, and the chariot was smashed. Ravana

---

*Ravana was known as an accomplished veena player.

parried and hit and used all the weapons in his command, but Jatayu kept up an unrelenting offensive.

Ravana tried to spare Jatayu up to a point. His anger finally rose and he took a special sword (an infallible one gifted to him by Shiva) called "Chandrahasa" and with a couple of flourishes and swings dealt a final blow to Jatayu, lopped off his gigantic wings, and pierced his throat. After Jatayu fell, Ravana picked himself up, abandoned his chariot, placed Sita on his shoulder with the piece of ground beneath her and, exercising his power to fly in the air, carried her off to Lanka.

Meanwhile Jatayu, with an effort of will, kept himself alive until Rama and Lakshmana, searching for Sita, came that way. With his dying breath, Jatayu gave an account of what he had witnessed and said, "Do not despair. You will succeed in the end." Rama anxiously asked, "In which direction did they go?" But Jatayu was dead before he could answer.

6

VALI

The perfect man takes a false step, apparently commits a moral slip, and we ordinary mortals stand puzzled before the incident. It may be less an actual error of commission on his part than a lack of understanding on ours; measured in Eternity, such an event might stand out differently. But until we attain that breadth of view, we are likely to feel disturbed and question the action. Rama was an ideal man, all his faculties in control in any circumstances, one possessed of an unwavering sense of justice and fair play. Yet he once acted, as it seemed, out of partiality, half-knowledge, and haste, and shot and destroyed, from hiding, a creature who had done him no harm, not even seen him. This is one of the most controversial chapters in the Ramayana.

The characters in the drama that follows are Vali, Sugreeva, Hanuman, and Rama. The action takes place in the mountainous forest regions of Kiskinda, a kingdom ruled and inhabited by monkeys. In the Ramayana, the participants are not only human beings but many others from God's creation, intelligent, cultured, and with their own achievements of spirit as well as physique: Jambavan was a bear, Jatayu was an eagle, Lakshmana—Rama's brother —was himself a human incarnation of the Great Serpent Adisesha in whose coils Vishnu rested. Whatever might be the form and shape, when they spoke and acted, their physical appearance passed unnoticed.

Kiskinda was peopled and ruled by what might broadly speaking be named a monkey race; but they were beings endowed with extraordinary intelligence, speech, immeasurable strength and nobility, and were of godly parentage too.

Rama, in his desperate quest of Sita, was journeying south-wards and crossed the frontiers of Kiskinda. Although he was an incarnation of Vishnu, the Supreme God, in human form, as we have seen, he was subject to human limitations of understanding and the despairs arising therefrom. Following Sita's trail by hearsay and hints, he and Lakshmana arrived on the frontiers of Kiskinda. Their entry was not unobserved. The companion and helper of Sugreeva, ruler of the monkey clan, was Hanuman, who will later take his place in the Ramayana as a major char-acter. Hanuman, watching for intruders, noticed Rama and Lakshmana far off on the mountain path. Assuming the shape of a young scholar, he went down and remained hidden behind a tree on their path. When they approached, he observed them closely and reflected within himself. "So noble-looking! Who are they? They are clad in tree bark, hair matted and knotted, ascetics. But they bear enormous bows on their shoulders. As-cetics armed like warriors or warriors clothed in ascetics' robes? But they still look like—like whom? They appear to be incom-parable beings. No way of judging by comparison. Are they gods?—but they look so human." Hanuman, unable to contain himself, stepped up before them and announced, "I am the son of Vayu and Anjana. I am called Anjaneya (or Hanuman), I am in the service of my chief, Sugreeva, who is the son of the sun god. I welcome you to our kingdom on his behalf."

Rama whispered to his brother, "Don't be misled by his ap-pearance. He looks like a youthful scholar, but he must be pos-sessed of great powers!" And then he said, "Please guide us to your chief."

Now Hanuman asked, "Whom shall I have the honour of an-nouncing?" While Rama paused, Lakshmana stepped in to say, "We are the sons of Dasaratha, the late King of Ayodhya." He narrated briefly their history and explained why they were here rather than at the palace in the capital city. On hearing the story, Anjaneya prostrated himself at the feet of Rama. Rama said, "No, you are a man of learning and I am only a warrior and you should not touch my feet," whereupon Hanuman (or An-janeya) said, "I assumed the scholar's form only for the purpose

of coming before you," and resumed his real stature and the
form of a giant monkey. He then left them, to return later ac-
companied by Sugreeva.

Rama, at the first sight of Sugreeva, felt an instinctive compas-
sion and also felt that this was a momentous encounter, a turning
point in his own life. Sugreeva, sensing his sympathetic attitude,
seized this occasion to mention his difficulties in a general way.
"Through no fault of mine, I suffer exile and privations."

"Have you lost your home and are you separated from your
wife?" When this question was asked, Sugreeva, too over-
whelmed to speak, remained silent. Whereupon Hanuman
stood up and told his story.

SUGREEVA'S STORY

Blessed by the grace of Shiva, there is one who possesses unlim-
ited strength and his name is Vali, the brother of Sugreeva here.
In ancient times, when the gods and demons tried to churn the
ocean to obtain nectar, using Mount Meru as a churning rod,
they were unable to move the churner. Vali, on an appeal by the
gods, pushed aside everyone and turned the churner until nectar
was obtained, which the gods consumed and which gave them
freedom from death. For this service Vali was rewarded with
immeasurable strength. He has more energy than the five ele-
ments in nature and at one stride could cross the seven oceans
and reach the mountain Charuvala, beyond all the seas. Also he
was blessed with this peculiar favour. Whoever approached him
for a fight lost half his strength to Vali, who thus enhanced his
own fighting powers.

Every day Vali visited all the eight directions, worshipped
Shiva in all his aspects. When he moved, he was faster than a
storm. No lance could pierce his chest. When he strode across
the earth the mountains shook, and the storm clouds parted and
dissipated themselves at his approach, afraid to precipitate rain.
All nature feared him. Even Yama was afraid to approach
where he and his armies camped. Thunder softened its voice,
and lions and other wild animals refrained from roaring in his

presence, and even the wind was afraid to shake down the leaves of trees. The ten-headed Ravana he once just pushed aside and tucked up in his tail.

Vali is elder to Sugreeva, possesses the resplendence and the cool complexion of the full moon. He is supreme and enforces his authority unquestioned like Yama himself. He was our King and Sugreeva was his next in authority. We were all happy under his rule. Then, as if to destroy the harmony of our whole existence, a demon called Mayavi—with protruding fangs and odious features—appeared in our midst and challenged Vali. The moment Vali rose to fight, Mayavi realized that he had been rash, and abruptly withdrew and fled beyond the edge of the world, into a subterranean passage. Vali chased him there determined to annihilate him.

Vali had left in a delirium of chase, but paused for a brief moment to tell Sugreeva, before disappearing into the netherworld, "Stay here and watch until I return." Twenty-eight months passed. There was no sign of Vali. No news. Sugreeva, distraught, decided to go into the tunnel in search of his brother. His counsellors and the elders around him, however, dissuaded him, saying that he could not abdicate his responsibility, which was to become the ruler of Kiskinda, as Vali must be presumed to be dead. They pushed up all the mountains over the mouth of the cavern in order to prevent, as they feared, Mayavi's possible return to attack Sugreeva also. They left a permanent body of sentries to watch that blocked entrance and installed Sugreeva as the ruler of Kiskinda.

But in due course there came out—not Mayavi but Vali. Vali had finally destroyed Mayavi and was now emerging victorious. He had tried the only exit and found it blocked with rolled-up mountains, which enraged him, as he thought that Sugreeva had been trying to seal him off underground. He kicked the obstacle aside and came out like a tornado. He reached Kiskinda. Sugreeva rose to welcome him and to express his joy at seeing him back. But Vali did not give him a chance to speak. He thundered, "So you thought you could entomb me?" and pounced on his brother and boxed and pounded him in the presence of all the courtiers and officials. Sugreeva could get no word in, nor bear the force of his attack. He still tried to speak and explain, but he could make no progress with his sentence, although he began several times: "The counsellors and elders . . ."

Vali seized Sugreeva and tried to smash him against a rock. Sugreeva managed to slip out of his hands and fled, but was mercilessly pursued by his brother, until, through a divine inspiration, he reached this mountain, called Mount Matanga, where Vali dare not step in. Sage Matanga has laid a curse on Vali for misdemeanour: that whenever Vali sets foot on this mountain, his skull will burst into fragments, and that none of the immunities granted to him will be effective here. So Sugreeva has sought refuge here, but the minute he steps out, Vali has sworn to kill him. When Vali went back, he not only resumed his authority as a ruler over the kingdom (which he had really not lost), but also forcibly acquired Sugreeva's wife and made her his own. And now Sugreeva has neither a home nor a wife.

*   *

Rama was moved by this story. He was filled with pity for Sugreeva and promised, "I will help you. Tell me what you want."

Sugreeva took Hanuman aside and asked, "What do you think of his offer of help?"

Hanuman replied, "I have not the slightest doubt that this person can vanquish Vali. Though he has not revealed his true self yet, I sense his identity. He could be none other than Vishnu himself. I notice that he has the marks of the Conch and the Disc in his palm. None but Vishnu could have bent the bow of Shiva and broken it, none but he could have set upon Thataka and her brood or revived Ahalya from her stony existence. More than all, my inner voice tells me who he is. When I was young, my father Vayu Bhagavan commanded me, 'You shall dedicate your life to the service of Vishnu.'

" 'How shall I know him?' I asked. He answered 'You will find him wherever evil is rampant—seeking to destroy it. Also, when you meet him, you will be filled with love and will not be able to move away from his presence.' Now I feel held to the presence of our visitor by some unknown power. I have no doubt who he is, but if you wish to test the power of his arrow, ask him to shoot at the trunk of one of these trees. If the shaft pierces and goes through, you may take it that he can send an arrow through Vali's heart."

They went back to Rama. Sugreeva requested Rama to give them proof of his archery. Rama said with a smile, "Yes, if it will help you. Show me the trees." They took him along to where seven trees stood in a row. They were enormous, older than the Vedas, and had survived four dissolutions of the universe. Their branches swept the heavens. No one, not even Brahma, could measure the distance between the top and bottom of these trees. Rama stood in front of the seven trees and twanged his bow string, the resonance echoing through all the hills and valleys. Then Rama took out an arrow and shot it through not only the trunks of the seven trees but also through the seven worlds, and the seven seas, and all things in seven; and then it returned to its starting point in the quiver. Sugreeva was overwhelmed at this demonstration and bowed his head in humility, convinced now that he was in the presence of a saviour.

On the top of this mountain Rama noticed a heap of bleached bones and asked Sugreeva, "What is that?" Sugreeva told him the story.

DUNDUBI'S STORY

These are the bones of a monster named Dundubi; he was a powerful demon in the shape of a buffalo. He had sought out Vishnu and said, "I wish to engage you in a war." Vishnu directed him to Shiva as the appropriate person for such an expedition. Dundubi went to Mount Kailas and tried to lift it off with his horn. Shiva appeared before him and asked, "You are shaking our foundation. What is your wish?" Dundubi said, "I want to fight forever. Please grant me that power." Shiva directed Dundubi to the chief of all the gods, Indra, who said, "Go down to the earth and meet Vali. He is the only one who can fulfill your ambition."

Accepting this advice, Dundubi came down and tried to destroy all this part of the earth, shouting foul challenges addressed to Vali. Vali attacked him. Their fight continued for one year without a break. Finally Vali plucked Dundubi's horn off his head and gored him to death and, lifting him by his neck, whirled him about and flung him high into the air; and the carcass flew through the sky, and fell down at this spot, where Sage Matanga was performing some sacred rites. The sage moved off after cursing Vali for defiling his prayer ground.

* *

Rama ordered Lakshmana, "Push away those bones," and Lakshmana kicked the whole heap out of sight, restoring to the spot its original sanctity.

Sugreeva now said, "I must tell you this; long ago we saw Ravana carrying off Sita in the skies. We were attracted by her screams and as we looked up, she bundled her jewellery and threw it down. Perhaps to indicate the way she passed"—and Sugreeva placed before Rama a bundle of jewellery. At the sight of it, Rama was grief-stricken. Tears came to his eyes and he swooned. Sugreeva revived him and promised, "I will not rest till I find where she is and restore her to you."

Rama grieved that he had not protected his wife—the ornaments reminding him again and again of his lapse. "Even a common stranger when he see a helpless woman taunted or ill treated will give his life to save her but I have failed to protect my wife, who trusted me implicitly and followed me into the wilderness; and I have failed her woefully." Thus he lamented, breaking down again and again.

Then Sugreeva and Hanuman spoke encouraging words. It was very moving to see a warrior and saviour in such a state of sorrow. Sugreeva and Hanuman elaborated the plan to trace Sita and recover her. Presently, the discussions grew into a council of war and they planned how they would set forth and search and not rest until Sita was found. Rama lamented, "Oh, human limitation that denies one the far-sight to know where, in which corner of the world or the heavens, that monster is holding Sita."

Hanuman spoke practically at this point. "First thing is to vanquish Vali. Sugreeva must be firmly established in his seat. Then we can gather our army. We need a big army for this task, as we must search simultaneously in every nook and corner and attack and overcome our enemy before rescuing the noble lady. So the first act to perform is to vanquish Vali. Let us go forth."

They went through forests and mountains, fragrant with sandalwood and other trees, and reached Kiskinda mountain. Rama said to Sugreeva, "You will now go forward alone and call out Vali for a fight. I will stand aside unseen and shoot my arrow into him at the right moment." Sugreeva had now full trust in Rama. He marched to the hilltop and shouted, "Oh, my brother Vali, come on, face me now in battle if you dare."

These words resounded through the silent forests and entered Vali's right ear while he slept. Vali sat up and laughed aloud. He got up with such force that the base of the mountain sank. His eyes spat fire, he ground his teeth in anger, slapped his thigh, clapped his hands, and the sound he made echoed through the valleys. "Yes, yes, here I come," shouted Vali rising from his bed. His voice resounded like thunder through the heavens, the ornaments around his neck snapped, scattering the gems.

Tara, his wife, interceded at this moment, pleading, "Please do not go out now. There must be some extraordinary reason why your brother is behaving in this manner."

Vali shouted, "Oh, my wife, get out of my way now. Sugreeva is just crazy through desperation and loneliness. That's all. Nothing so serious as you fear. You'll see me come back in a moment, drunk with the blood of that brother of mine."

"He would not ordinarily dare to come your way but I fear now he must be having some mighty support, which encourages him to challenge you now. So be careful."

"Dear wife, if all the creatures in all the worlds oppose me, I can face them and wipe them out. That you know very well. You who have the elegance of a peacock and the voice of a nightingale, listen, have you forgotten that whoever confronts me gives me half his strength—how can anyone escape me? It's only some senseless creature who would offer support to my brother."

And now Tara quietly mentioned, "Some persons who are interested in our welfare have told me of a rumour that one Rama has moved into these parts, and he is Sugreeva's ally. Rama bears an invincible bow, and it has given new hope to Sugreeva."

"Oh, foolish creature, you are betraying a woman's intelligence and a gossiping tongue. You are uttering a blasphemy for which I would have killed anyone else. But I spare you. You've committed a grievous error of judgement and speech. I know about Rama—more than you do. I have my own sources of knowledge about what goes on in the world outside. I have heard of Rama as being one possessing integrity and a sense of justice; one who could never take a wrong step. How could you ever imagine that such a person would ever take sides in a quarrel between brothers? Do you know that he renounced his right to the throne and undertook the penance of a forest life, all because he wished to see his father's ancient promises fulfilled? Instead of uttering his name reverently, how can you slander him? Even if all the worlds oppose him, he needs no strength other than his own "Kodanda," his great bow. Would he count on the support of a miserable monkey like Sugreeva—even if you assume that he expects to rescue his wife through Sugreeva's help? One who has gifted away his birthright to a younger brother, would he ever employ his prowess to take sides in a family quarrel among strangers? Stay here, my beloved, and don't move; within the twinkling of an eye, I will be back after disposing of the nuisance named Sugreeva."

Afraid to contradict her husband any further, Tara stood aside to let him pass. Swollen with the zest for fight, his figure looked redoubled and struck terror into those who beheld him. As Vali stepped on the arena at the mountainside, uttering a variety of challenges and shouts, all creatures that heard him stood arrested, stunned and deafened.

Beholding the stature of Vali, Rama whispered to his brother Lakshmana, "Is there any comparable spectacle of power in the whole universe, even if you include all the gods, demons, and the elements?"

Lakshmana had his misgivings. "I am not certain whether Sug-reeva is trying to involve you in anything more than an ordinary combat between mere monkeys. I do not know if we should participate in this struggle at all. How can you trust as an ally one who has not hesitated to intrigue fatally against a brother?"

"Why limit it to monkeys? Strife between brothers is common among human beings too. Instances like Bharatha's are rare indeed. We should not become too analytical about a friend, nor look too deeply into original causes; but accept only what appears good to us in the first instance, and act on it."

While they were thus discussing, Vali and Sugreeva clashed. Then they separated, dodged, and went at each other again. When their shoulders or feet rubbed together, blinding sparks flew off. Sparks flew from their eyes. They drew blood from each other by scratching and tearing and gashing; the air was filled with their roars and challenges and the resounding blows delivered to each other. They tried to coil their mighty tails and press the life out of each other. It was impossible to judge in their entanglement who was gaining or losing.

Finally Sugreeva was fisted, kicked, mauled, and beaten so badly that he withdrew baffled and paralysed. He found a pause and approached Rama and gasped: "Help me, I can't bear it any more. . . ." Rama said, "While you are at grips with each other, it is impossible to know who is who; and I don't want to shoot you by mistake. Why don't you pluck that wild creeper with its flowers and garland it around your neck, so that I can identify you while you whirl tempestuously about? Now go back to your fight." Sugreeva immediately tore off a wild creeper which was hanging down a tree branch, put it on as a garland, returned to the fray with renewed hope and vigour, and fell on Vali with a thunderous shout. Vali, pounding down with his fists and feet, with derisive laughter, returned the blow and hit Sugreeva in the vital centres of his life. Sugreeva had little doubt now that his end had come, and threw a desperate glance in the direction of Rama. At this moment Vali grappled him by his neck and waist, lifted him over his head in order to dash him against a rock and end his career. Rama drew an arrow elegantly from his quiver, poised it on the bow-string, and let it go. It sped along and pierced Vali's chest like a needle passing through a fruit.

Overcome with astonishment, Vali paused for a moment to take stock of the situation. His grip around his brother's neck relaxed involuntarily. With one hand he had held on to the arrows shaft and arrested its passage through his chest. Now he clung to it with his hands, his feet, and the coils of his tail, and broke and retarded its motion with such stubborn strength that even Yama, the god of death, stood back, nodding his head in admiration.

Vali had never thought, even as a possibility, that there was any power on earth or in the heavens which could subdue him with any weapon or stand up before him in a fight. All this was an accepted fact, but here he was like a miserable worm, not even able to understand what it was that had laid him low. Could it be the "Trisula" of Shiva or could it be the "Chakra" of Vishnu or Indra's "Vajrayudha"? He laughed ironically. At the same moment he felt an admiration for the unknown assailant. Who could it be? he speculated, forgetting his pain. He was invulnerable according to the promise of the gods, yet here was the reality, the arrow in his heart. He laughed bitterly at his own cocksureness of these years; what could it be, who could it be? Why speculate? Let me find out. So saying he exercised all his remaining strength in pulling the arrow from his chest, to look at the mark on its handle. The might of Vali was applauded by the gods watching from high heavens, as he succeeded in drawing out the shaft. Blood gushed from the wound like a spring. At the sight of it, Sugreeva was grief-stricken and wept aloud. He forgot his animosity. With his ebbing strength, Vali held the arrow close to his eyes and spelt the name "Rama" engraved on it. Vali looked at the name on the arrow and almost was blinded with shock. The shock of the physical injury was not so agonizing as the spiritual shock of reading the name of Rama on the arrow. He looked at it and brooded over his own recklessness in castigating his wife for mentioning Rama's name. That poor creature showed better judgement than he.

"Rama, the Lord of culture, breeding, discrimination, and

justice. How could you do this? You have destroyed the firm ba-
sis of your own virtues. Is it because of the separation from your
wife that you have lost all sense of fairness and act recklessly? If
some demon like Ravana has acted treacherously, is that any jus-
tification for you to come here, slaughter the head of a monkey
clan, entirely unconnected with the affair? Has your code of
ethics taught you only this? What mistake have you seen in me,
young man, that you should destroy me thus? Who will wear the
badge of virtue in this world or others, when you have thrown it
away so lightly? Is the foretaste of the *yuga* of *Kali** to be had
only by us, the creatures who crawl and are called monkeys? So,
Kind One, are virtues intended to be practised only on weaker
creatures? When strong men commit crimes, they become heroic
deeds? Oh, incomparable one, the treasure and the kingdom
given to you, you handed over to the younger brother. That you
performed in the city; do you wish to repeat a similar act in
these forests too by depriving an older brother of his life and
kingdom? When two persons are opposed to each other, how
can you in support of one, hide and attack the other? What you
have done to me is not heroic or an act conducted within the
laws of warfare. Surely, you do not consider me a burden on this
weighty earth nor are you my enemy. Pray, tell me what drove
you to this terrible decision? Ravana entrapped your wife and
carried her off. To redeem her and to wreak your vengeance on
him, you probably seek the support of Sugreeva, which is like
courting a rabbit, when you can summon a lion to serve you.
Pray what judgement is this? A word from you and I'd have
plucked Ravana from his citadel and flung him at your feet.

   "You have done a thing which has ended my life. If someone
has carried away your wife, instead of battling with him face to

---

* "Each yuga lasts for 3000 years, by celestial measurements; but one celestial
year is the equivalent of 3600 years of human time, so that the four yugas cover
a span of 43,200,000 mortal years. Each of the four yugas . . . possesses spe-
cial characteristics of good and evil. . . . In *Kaliyuga* righteousness, virtue, and
goodness completely disappear. Rites and sacrifices are abandoned as mere su-
perstitions. Anger, distress, hunger, and fear prevail, and rulers behave like
highwaymen, seizing power and riches in various ways." *Gods, Demons, and
Others.*

face, you stand aside, hide, and use all your accomplishment as an archer against an unarmed stranger. Has all your training as a warrior been only for this end? Creatures like us test our worth and strength with our sinews and muscles and always fight barehanded, and never hold a weapon as you do."

Rama softly came out of his hiding, approached the dying Vali, and said with the utmost calmness, "When you disappeared into the subterranean world pursuing Mayavi, your brother waited in anxiety for a very long time, and then on a sudden resolve, started to follow your path into the tunnel since he feared that you might need help. But he was held back by the army chiefs and advisers in your court, who pressed him to rule as a trustee for the time being. But the moment you came back, you misunderstood everything and before he could even express his relief and joy on seeing you, you belaboured him mercilessly in the presence of the others and attempted to take his life. When he still struggled to explain and sought your pardon for any mistake on his part, you rejected his appeal. And then even after fully realizing that he had committed no wrong, you let your temper carry you on and on; you could afford, through your sense of power, to indulge your anger luxuriously, however unwarranted; and you assaulted and pursued him with the intention of killing him. After he fled, you left him alone, not because he had admitted his error and sought your pardon and asylum, and not even because it was wrong to pursue one whose back is turned in fight, not because he was your brother, but only because you dare not step on Matanga's Hill—merely self-preservation. And you bided your time. Even now you would have squeezed his life out but for my arrow. Beyond all this, you violated his wife's honour and made her your own. Guarding a woman's honour is the first duty laid on any intelligent being. But because you are conscious of your limitless strength, you act dishonourably and carry it off without any compunction as you feel no one can question you. You are well versed in the laws of conduct and morality and yet instead of affording protection to a helpless woman, life partner of a brother at that, you have molested her.

"Since Sugreeva sought my friendship and asked for help, I felt it my duty to help him by destroying you."

Vali replied, "You are judging us all wrongly, your basis is mistaken. You make too much of my acquiring my brother's wife. It's legitimate in our society. Although my brother was an enemy, I wanted to protect and help his wife when he was gone. I could not leave her to her fate."

"It is my primary duty to help the weak and destroy evil wherever I see it. Whether known or unknown, I help those that seek my help."

Vali replied, "Marriage and all its restraints on the relationship of men and women are of your human society and not known to us. Brahma has decreed for us absolute freedom in our sexual pursuits, habits, and life. In our society there is no such thing as wedlock. We are not a human society, we are monkeys and your laws and ethical codes are not applicable to us."

"I am not misled either by your explanation or appearance of being a monkey," Rama said. "I am aware that you are begotten by the chief of gods. You possess enough intelligence to know right from wrong and to argue your case even at this stage. You are fully aware of the eternal verities. You have erred and know it and how can you now say you are innocent? Could Gajendra, who prayed for Vishnu's help when a crocodile held him in its jaws, be classed as an ordinary elephant? Could Jatayu be called a common bird? An ordinary animal has no discrimination between right and wrong. But you display in your speech deep knowledge of life's values. Creatures in human shape may be called animals if they display no knowledge of right and wrong and conversely so-called animals which display profundity cease to be animals and will have to be judged by the highest standards. There can be no escape from it. It was through your steadfast meditation and prayer to Shiva that you were endowed with strength superior to even the five elements. One who is capable of such achievement cannot but be judged by the highest standards of conduct."

"Very well," said Vali, "I'll accept what you say; but how could you, protector of all creatures, aim your shaft from your hiding place, like some mean hunter tracking a wild

beast, instead of facing me in a fight—if you felt that I de-
served that honour?"

Lakshmana gave the answer. "Rama had made a vow to sup-
port your brother Sugreeva when he came seeking refuge. This
was a prior promise and had to be fulfilled, while if Rama had
come before you face to face you might have made a similar ap-
peal, which would have created confusion of purpose. That's
the reason why he shot unseen by you."

Vali saw the inner purport of this explanation and said,
"Now I understand your words differently from the way they
sound. They are simple to hear but have inner strength and I
feel assured that Rama has not committed an unrighteous act.
Simple-minded ones like me can never realize eternal truths
without constantly blundering and failing. Pray, forgive my er-
rors and my rude speech. Instead of treating me as a mere mon-
key by birth, as I myself was content to think, you have elevated
my status, and honoured me. After piercing my body with your
arrow, and when I am about to die—you are touching my un-
derstanding with a supreme illumination, which I consider the
greatest blessing ever conferred on me. In spite of my obstinacy
you have helped me attain a profound understanding and opened
my mind with your magic. While other gods confer boons after
being asked, you confer them on the mere utterance of your
name. Great sages have attempted, after aeons of austerities, to
obtain a vision of God, but you have bestowed it on me
unasked. I feel proud and happy at this moment. I have only
one request. I hope my brother will prove worthy of your trust
in him. But at any time if any weakness seizes him and you find
him in the wrong, please do not send your arrow in his direc-
tion. Treat him kindly.

"Another thing. If your brothers, at any time, blame Sugreeva
as one who had engineered the death of his brother, please ex-
plain to them that Sugreeva has only engineered my salvation.
One more favour. I have not been blessed with a chance to
pluck up that archfiend Ravana with the tip of my tail and place
him before you. But here is Hanuman who will do it at your
command, and also obey you in all matters. Let him serve you.
Sugreeva and he will be your invaluable allies."

Then he turned to Sugreeva. "Don't sorrow for my death. He who has struck me is none other than the great God himself; and I realize I am a privileged being at this moment. You will always have the glory of being at his side, and please serve him well." Then Vali formally handed Sugreeva over to Rama as his choice for succession and advised him as to how to rule.

This is the saddest part of our great epic. The lamentations of Tara and Angada, Vali's wife and son, as they came down carrying the dead body of the mighty Vali, make one's heart grow heavy. But all stories must have a happy ending. Though Tara clung to the inert lifeless Vali's physical frame, his essential spirit soared to the highest heavens and found a place there, because the great God himself had released his soul. On the command of Rama, arrangements were begun for the coronation of Sugreeva, and Angada was made the *yuvaraja* or second in command.

7

WHEN THE RAINS CEASE

Sugreeva was crowned with elaborate rituals and festivities. Robed royally, and wearing a scintillating crown, Sugreeva approached Rama, who had stayed outside Kiskinda throughout the celebrations, and declared in a mood of deep gratitude, "I am ready to serve you, sir. What is your command?"

Rama put his arms around his shoulder tenderly and said, "Go back to your palace and to your tasks as a ruler." Following the custom of a senior, he spoke a few words of advice: "Gather around yourself those that have integrity, courage, and judgement; and with their help govern your subjects. Whatever you do, let it be based on the sanctioned codes of conduct." He explained how he should guard the interests of his subjects, how important gentleness in speech was: "Even when you realize that the one before you is an enemy and must be treated sternly, do not hurt with words. Even in jest, do not hurt anyone's feelings, not even the lowliest," he said—remembering how he used to make fun of Kooni's deformity when he was young and fling balls of clay at her, and thinking that possibly Kooni had nursed her ill will all her life and found her opportunity for revenge when Dasaratha planned to enthrone him. Rama explained how even a trivial cause might bring disaster in its wake. He then expatiated on how far one should surrender one's own judgement to another—especially out of love. "Not too far," he said, referring to his own pursuit of the golden deer in order to please Sita. "Women can lead one to death," he said, referring to Vali's infatuation with Sugreeva's wife. At the conclusion of their meeting, Sugreeva pleaded, "Please do me the honour of residing as our guest in the capital."

Rama said, "Not now. If you have me as a guest, all your attention will be on me, while you should devote your energy to your duties as a king. Moreover, I have vowed to live in the forests for fourteen years and I cannot, therefore, come into a city now."

Sugreeva was crestfallen, and said, "I want to serve you. . . ."

"Yes, later. The rainy season is coming. At the end of it, come with an army. There will be time enough."

Anjaneya now said stubbornly, "I have no existence separated from you. I want to serve you. I wish to be with you forever."

Rama said, "Not now. You will go back to Kiskinda with Sugreeva and help him. He will need your judgement and support, as the responsibilities he has inherited are immense. Your first duty will be to help him. Come to me after four months, after the rains, and I will tell you what you can do for me." When Sugreeva still pressed his invitation, Rama said, "I have lost my wife; and I should not be said to be enjoying the luxuries of a palace, when perhaps she is undergoing untold suffering somewhere." After sending away Sugreeva and Hanuman, Rama turned back with Lakshmana, to reside on a hill. At a chosen spot, Lakshmana, displaying again his genius as an architect, constructed an ashram—in which they could spend the coming rainy months and where Rama could serenely contemplate his future course of action.

The sun began to move southward. Dark clouds, heavily laden, floated along, frequently eclipsing the sun, gradually massing themselves like an army of gigantic elephants; thunders rumbled and roared, lightning lit up the sky and the earth end to end. Storm shook the trees, ripped off their foliage, and scattered it in the air; scoured the earth and sprayed up mud and dust. Just as we felt the total heat and aridity where Thataka used to roam, now we must feel under our skin the dampness, the dimness, and the apparent lifelessness of the rainy days.

All through the months, the rains poured, waters running, rushing, and stagnating in pools, and sometimes carrying down boulders or the portion of a mountainside. Cuckoos and nightingales were silent. Peacocks were unseen. Other creatures of the forest were incarcerated in stony recesses and caves. No animal

stirred out. No movement. Every kind of life seemed to have be-
come paralysed. Wild and uncouth vegetation overran the land-
scape in a variety of monstrous creepers and vines. The sky was
perpetually overcast. Winds blew cold and damp and drenched
one's surroundings and person. For a few days, the change of
season was fascinating, but, in course of time, the persistent
gloom and wetness proved depressing.

Rama, isolated in this climate, became subject to long periods
of melancholy. The surrounding conditions made his inner tur-
moil more acute. He now felt hopelessly cut off from his wife
and no action to seek her ever seemed possible. He felt thwarted
and desolate. He began to feel guilty; he thought he was being
too complacent. "While I live sheltered here, I cannot imagine
what misery she might be facing." When he saw foaming, froth-
ing, reddish floodwater rushing down the mountain, bearing
and rolling along uprooted trees, he was reminded of Sita being
carried off. It created a hopeless ache in his heart and he said to
himself, "There is no meaning in my continuing to live." When
he saw streaks of lightning splitting the sky, he pictured them as
the monstrous fangs of asuras grinning and menacing him on
all sides, and he pleaded, "Just when one of your clan has taken
away the very core of my life, you want to take more? Nothing
more is left." When he saw an occasional deer emerge from its
shelter when the downpour slackened a little, he addressed it,
"You were jealous of Janaki; she was your rival in the grace of
her movements. Now are you not pleased that she is no longer
here? One of your kind drew me away from her. Now what is
your purpose in strutting before me?" When he saw a slender
streak of lightning edging a cloud, he sighed, "Why should you
remind me of Sita's figure and vanish again? When you rumble,
does it signify your determination to restore Sita to me?" Then
he addressed the god of love, Manmatha: "You are a tormentor.
I feel scorched, and while I seek something to heal me, your
darts stab again and again the same sore spot at my heart—
merciless god! It is your good fortune that you are unseen,
which saves you; my brother would have eliminated you, if he
had seen how you torture me. Do you know what happened to
Soorpanaka?"

Lakshmana noticed Rama's state of mind and felt it was time for him to comfort him. He said, "Are you worried that the rainy days are prolonged? Are you worried that the asuras might prove invincible? Do you fear that Janaki may not be traced at all? Please don't let your mind weaken. Anjaneya is there, Angada and all the other stalwarts will be our helpers. Soon we will see the skies bright and clear. Time has been passing, and we will soon see the promised armies, and with ease they will bring Janaki to your side. You had assured the sages of Dandaka forest that you would eradicate the asuras from their midst and that has been your chief mission here. Muster your strength and fulfill your mission. Don't let your spirit droop." Rama was comforted by such words, and they sustained him through a second bout of rain which suddenly started after a brief interval of clear weather.

The rains ended at last. The skies cleared. New leaves appeared on the trees; jasmine and other fragrant flowers bloomed. With brighter surroundings, Rama's spirit also quickened. Now he could move out of his ashram and act positively.

With the end of the rainy season, nature's traffic resumed on land, air, and water. Flocks of swans crossed the sky; cranes and aquatic birds flew by; a variety of fishes newly spawned darted under the water surfaces. Lotus was in bloom; frogs which had croaked themselves hoarse in unison all through the wet days now were silent. Peacocks came out into the sun shaking off clogging droplets of water and fanning out their tails brilliantly. Rivers which had roared and overflowed now retraced their modest courses and tamely ended in the sea. Areca palms ripened their fruits in golden bunches; crocodiles emerged from the depths crawling over rocks to bask in the sun; snails vanished under slush, and crabs slipped back under ground; that rare creeper known as *vanji* suddenly burst into bloom with chattering parrots perched on its slender branches.

All this was minutely noted by Rama, as indicating a definite change of season and a reminder that Sugreeva had failed to keep his promise to arrive with his army. He said to Lakshmana, "Does it not seem that Sugreeva has exceeded the four months' limit? Do you think he is asleep? With our help, he has acquired a mighty kingdom to rule, but he has forgotten us. One who has snapped all ties of friendship, swerved from truth, and acted false, deserves to be taught a lesson, and if he is killed in the process, we could not be blamed; but first of all will you go and find out why he has defaulted, what has happened to him, and if he deserves to be punished? You will tell him that destroying evil is like destroying a poisonous insect and we will not be violating any code of conduct thereby. You will explain with due clarity and impress it on the mind of one who does not seem to have known proper conduct either at five years of age or at fifty. Tell him that if he wishes to flourish as a ruler of this Kiskinda in the midst of his kinsmen and people, he must first come up immediately with all the help he can muster to search for Sita. If he does not, we will not hesitate to destroy every monkey in this world, so that that tribe will become un-known to future generations. In case he has found someone stronger than Rama or Lakshmana as his supporters, remind him that we could meet any challenge from anywhere." After relieving his mood and temper with these words, Rama proba-bly felt that he had gone too far and might provoke Lakshmana to act violently. So he told him now, "Speak gently. Do not show your anger but let your explanations be firm and clear. If he does not accept the moral you indicate, do not lose your pa-tience but give a careful hearing to whatever he may have to say and bring me his reply."

Properly armed, Lakshmana left immediately. He was over-whelmed with the seriousness of his mission, and his mind was fixed on reaching his destination in the shortest time possible. He moved swiftly, looking neither to his left nor right. He avoided a familiar path leading to Kiskinda, the old pathway trodden by them when Sugreeva went forth to encounter Vali. Now Lakshmana, feeling uncertain about their relationship with Sugreeva, chose a different route. It was also a measure of precaution as he did not wish to be observed by Sugreeva's spies. He reached Kiskinda leaping along from crag to crag.

Observers at the outpost went to Angada with the news of Lakshmana's arrival. Angada hastened out to meet him, but even from a distance understood what temper he was in, and withdrew quietly; he rushed to Sugreeva's palace, which had been designed and built by a master architect and was so gorgeous and comfortable that Sugreeva hardly ever left it. His bed chamber was strewn with flowers, and he lay surrounded by beauties with long tresses and heavy breasts, who provided his comforts, and sang and entertained him. The company of beautiful women, with their dizzying perfumes and the scent of flowers and rare incense, and above all much wine imbibed, left him in a daze of ecstasy. Sugreeva lay inert, unmindful of the world outside; Angada softly entered, respectfully saluted his recumbent uncle, and whispered, "Listen to me, please. Rama's brother Lakshmana is come; in his face I see anger and urgency. What is your command to me now?"

There was no response from Sugreeva. As he gave no sign of comprehending his words, Angada left, went in search of Hanuman, consulted him, and took him along to meet his mother, Tara. He explained to his mother what had happened and appealed to her for guidance. She lost her temper and cried, "You have all indulged in wrong acts without thinking of morality or the consequences. You gain your ends and then forget your responsibilities. You do not possess gratitude. I have dinned into you again and again that the time has come to help Rama; but it seemed as if I were talking to a stone wall. Now you must suffer the consequences of your indifference. You do not realize how Rama is bearing up and how hard it must be for him to remain alive at all. You are all lost in pleasures. You are all selfish and ungrateful. You are prosperous, with no thought for others. You now ask what you should do. You will all perish if you plan to wage a war on Rama and Lakshmana. What is there for me to advise you?"

When she said this, the populace of Kiskinda shut and bolted the city gates and barricaded them with rocks and tree-trunks. Lakshmana watched them, both irritated and amused, and then, with a push and a kick, shattered the blockade and flung the gates open. Great confusion ensued; the monkey populace fled into the neighbouring forests, deserting the city. Lakshmana stepped majestically into the city and looked about. Angada and all the others who stood surrounding Tara, observing him from a distance, asked themselves anxiously, "What shall we do now?"

At this moment, Hanuman counselled Tara, "Please move onto the threshold of the palace with your attendants. Lakshmana will not go past you. Otherwise, I dread to think what might happen if he rushes into the palace."

"All of you now leave," Tara said, "and remain out of sight. I will go and face him."

By the time Lakshmana had traversed the royal path and reached the palace, he heard the jingle of anklets and bracelets, looked up, and discovered an army of women approaching him with determination. Before he could decide whether he should retreat, he found himself encircled; he felt confused and embarrassed. He bowed his head, unable to face anyone, and stood with downcast eyes wondering what to do.

Tara addressed him with all courtesy. "We are honoured and happy at your visit. But the manner of your coming has frightened us. Until we know what you have in mind, we will feel uneasy. Is there anything you wish to tell us?" she asked sweetly.

Lakshmana looked up, and at the first glimpse of Tara's face felt a sharp remembrance of his mother Sumithra and his stepmother Kausalya. Uncontrollably, his eyes filled with tears. For a moment he was assailed with homesickness. He overcame it and said, "I am sent by my brother to find out why Sugreeva has held himself back, having promised to bring an army for our help."

Tara replied, "Don't let your anger turn on Sugreeva. Great ones should forgive the lapses of small men. Anyway, Sugreeva has not forgotten. He has sent messages to all his associates, far and wide, in order to mobilize an army, and he is awaiting the return of the messengers, which is the only cause of delay. Please bear with us. We know that Rama's single arrow is enough to vanquish all enemies, and our help could only be nominal."

On hearing these words, Lakshmana looked relieved; noticing the signs of good temper, Hanuman approached him cautiously, and Lakshmana asked him, "Did you, too, forget your promise?"

Hanuman explained, "My mind is always fixed on Rama and there can be no forgetfulness." He spoke with such humility and sincerity that Lakshmana's anger finally left him. He now explained, "Rama's suffering is deep. He needs Sugreeva's help at this stage; and fears that the longer he delays, the stronger the evil-doers may grow." Hanuman said, "Please step into the palace and give Sugreeva a chance to receive you, sir. When you stand here refusing to enter, it gives a chance for our enemies to gossip and talk ill of us. Please forget the past and come in."

Accepting the invitation, Lakshmana followed him into the palace, and was received by Angada, who immediately went in to announce his arrival to Sugreeva. Meanwhile, Tara withdrew with her companions. Angada announced to Sugreeva that Lakshmana was there, and explained in what temper he had arrived and how the gates of the city fell at his touch. Sugreeva listened in surprise and demanded to be told why no one had informed him of Lakshmana's arrival in proper time. Angada replied gracefully, avoiding any direct charge, "I came in several times and spoke, but perhaps you were asleep when I thought you were awake."

"You are very considerate to explain it this way," Sugreeva said, "but I was drunk, and that made me forget my responsibilities and promises. Wine saps away one's energy, senses, judgement, and memory; and promises are lost sight-of; one loses even the distinction between one's wife and mother. We are already born into a world of Maya, born in a state of complete self-delusion; we add to this state further illusions that wine creates. No salvation for us. We turn a deaf ear to the advice of wise men and the lessons they point out, and instead just skim out the dirt and insects swimming in the fermented froth, quaff the drink and sink into oblivion. How can I face Lakshmana now?" He brooded for a little while and then declared, "I hereby vow in the name of the most sacred Rama that I will never drink any intoxicant again."

After this resolution, he felt braced up. "I will now receive Lakshmana. Meanwhile let all honours be properly presented to him and let there be public celebrations in his honour." Angada busied himself to set the wheels in motion; by the time

Sugreeva with his entourage sallied forth to meet Lakshmana, the atmosphere had changed into one of festivity, with the public participating fully in the reception. Music, chantings, incense, and flowers were everywhere and Sugreeva looked majestic.

At the first sight of Sugreeva, Lakshmana's anger revived for a second, but he suppressed it resolutely, clasped Sugreeva's hand, and entered the palace hall. Sugreeva pointed to a golden seat and invited Lakshmana to occupy it. Lakshmana merely said, "Rama sits on the bare ground; I don't need anything more than that." So saying he sat on the bare floor, an act which saddened Sugreeva and the others. Sugreeva next suggested, "Will you have a bath and partake of our repast?" Once again Lakshmana said, "Rama lives on roots and greens; so do I. Every minute I delay here, he will be going without food. Immediately start a search for Sita and that will be equal to giving me a holy bath in Ganga and offering me a dinner of ambrosia."

Sugreeva replied in great sorrow, "When Rama is suffering such privations, only a monkey like me can be lost in physical enjoyment. Forgive me." He turned next to Hanuman and said, "Our messengers have not arrived. When they return with the armies, bring them to Rama's ashram. Stay here until then. I will now go." He gathered his followers and proceeded to meet Rama, marching on in solemn silence, his mind full of guilt. But the moment he came face to face with Rama at his mountain retreat, Rama welcomed him with open arms, patted his back, and said, "I hope you and your subjects are happy and flourishing."

Sugreeva replied, "For one who has received your grace, the achievements of kingship seem trivial and light." He felt unable to stop his speech and became passionately self-critical: "I have failed in my duty, in my promise, lost myself in pleasures. I have betrayed the limits of the monkey mind. I do not have the right to expect your forgiveness."

"The rainy season was unexpectedly prolonged," Rama said, "and I knew that you must have been waiting for its close. Now your speech indicates your determination to help, which makes me happy. I do not doubt your devotion, but you must not belittle yourself so much. . . . Where is Hanuman?"

"He will come presently, with an army."

"Now you may go," Rama said; "you must have other duties to perform. Come back when the armies are ready." Sugreeva replied, "So be it. We shall decide on the details of our campaign later."

After he left, Rama received from Lakshmana a full report of all that he had seen and heard during his mission to Kiskinda.

In due course, various units, led by their commanders, appeared in the valley. In order to get an idea of their numbers, Sugreeva suggested that Rama stand at a height and watch, and ordered the commanders to parade their contingents one by one north to south. Rama's hopes revived as he watched the marchers disappear troop after troop into an enormous cloud of dust raised by their feet. He said to Lakshmana, "I try, but constantly lose count of the numbers. If we stand here and try to count, we will never reach the end of it, or have any time left to search for Sita. Now that we have seen this army, I am confident of their ability to search and fight." He turned to Sugreeva and said, "Now do not delay, get them into action."

Sugreeva called up the commanders and allotted to each a task, in different directions. Hanuman and Angada were to proceed southward, and that was the most important of the assignments. Before Hanuman departed, Sugreeva gave him detailed instructions as to how to search for Sita in each place they would be traversing.

"When you leave here you will reach the cloud-topping Vindhya mountain peaks," he continued. "Search for Sita in every nook and corner of that mountain range. Then you will cross the river Narmada, in whose cool waters even the gods will be sporting. Then you will reach the range called Hemakuta on whose gold-topped towers divine damsels descend, to spend their hours composing and singing lyrics which lull even birds and beasts to sleep. Leave Hemakuta and go farther south. Let your search everywhere be swift. You will come upon Vidarbha, with its frontiers marked with sandalwood and other fragrant trees, and a country of orchards of all the fruits nature can offer. Let not your army tarry here for a feast." Thus he

went on giving precise instructions for Hanuman's passage
through several parts of the country, giving a clear picture of
the landscape, mountains, valleys, and rivers to be crossed so
that the army might proceed on the right lines and not get lost.
Finally he said, "Do not let any holy spot divert your attention
from your main task. If you find yourself approaching that holi-
est mountain, Thiruvengadam, make a detour; a visit to this
spot will doubtless give you salvation, but seek your salvation
later after Sita has been found. Ravana is not likely to have set
foot on this sacred ground. Your time is limited. I will give you
thirty days to search. Soonest after that, I want you back here
with your report."

Anjaneya was ready to depart, but at this moment Rama
asked, "O learned one! If you come upon her, by what signs
will you recognize her as Sita?" Hanuman had no answer for
this. Whereupon Rama took him aside to explain, "If you ob-
serve her feet, you will find her toe-nails glowing red like ruby.
Her feet are incomparable. Observe her heels carefully. Learned
men have compared them to the quiver. I will not describe to
you her waist, which is, as it should be, delicate and unseen." It
gave him a peculiar relief to recollect Sita's features in detail
and describe them to Hanuman. Hanuman absorbed with re-
spectful attention every word of Rama's, without interrupting
him in any manner. Rama succeeded in creating a complete pic-
ture of Sita in Anjaneya's mind, and Anjaneya began to feel that
he was going in search of someone he had already known.
In addition to her features, Rama gave an account of how she
spoke, how she walked, what her voice would sound like, and
so on. "When you have seen this person and if your conscience
witnesses to it that she is the one and only person, approach
her, observe the state of her mind and talk to her. Ask if she re-
members how I saw her first on the terrace of Janaka's palace
on that evening when I passed along the road in the company of
my master Viswamithra. Did she not say later that if the one
who had snapped Shiva's bow was other than the one she saw
below her balcony in the company of Viswamithra she would
give up her life? Did she not enter the hall of assembly at her fa-
ther's palace, decked in jewellery, and anxiously glance up to

know if it was I or someone else? Remind her that when we started out on our exile, we had hardly reached the towering gates of Ayodhya, when she inquired innocently, 'Where are the cruel, impossible forests that you spoke of?'" After this series of messages, Rama took the ring from his finger and said, "Give this to her. May your mission conclude successfully."

Hanuman and Angada went southward, taking a picked army with them. They crossed mountains and rivers. Wherever they suspected Ravana might be hiding, they fell to in a frenzy and ransacked every nook and corner searching for Sita. In their desperation to find a shelter where she might be hidden, they rushed into the mouth of a cavern and, proceeding along a tunnel, found it impossible to get out: they were trapped in complete darkness. They lost trace of all directions, landmarks, forms, and outlines in an all-consuming darkness. They had no doubt that Ravana had contrived this for them, and felt helpless against a trickery designed to deprive them of their vision. Hanuman, through his extraordinary powers, helped them to edge their way along, until they found themselves led, deep within the bowels of the earth, after many an hour's journeying, to an enchanting city of palatial buildings, squares, fountains, parks, and avenues. Although no sunlight could pierce so deep, there was an unchanging glow emanating from the brilliant golden domes, embedded with precious stones emitting a natural light. With all this perfection, there was not a soul in sight. No human or any being of any kind anywhere. "Are we all dead and opening our eyes in heaven or is this another illusion that Ravana has created for us? If we are dead, how are we to discharge our duties to Rama? If we are alive, how are we to get out of this trap?"

Their problems were answered presently when they saw a woman sitting cross-legged lost in meditation—the sole occupant of this vast city. At first the monkeys mistook her for Sita, thinking that Ravana had obviously found the perfect concealment for her in the depths of the earth. But observing her closely, Hanuman declared that she did not bear any of the marks Rama had mentioned for identification. They woke the woman from her meditation and when she narrated her story they found that she had been a goddess, who for some mistake committed had fallen from grace and had been condemned to dwell underground in this perfect setting, in complete solitude, precisely until this moment. After her long penance she feasted and entertained Hanuman and his followers; finally, through Hanuman's own powers, they were able to shatter this underworld and come out, and also help this strange woman to escape from her imprisonment and go back to her own heaven.

They journeyed southward, leaving no stone unturned along the way, and reached the southernmost point of a mountaintop, where they watched the rolling ocean beyond and spoke among themselves: "There is nothing more for us to do. We have failed. We have long passed the one-month time limit. Should we renounce the world and stay on here as ascetics or take poison and end our lives, the only alternatives left for us?"

Angada said, "When we started out, we were boastful in Rama's presence. Now how can we go back and face him? We cannot return and report our failure. We may ask for more time but what shall we do with more time? If Rama asks what we are doing further, how shall we answer him? I cannot bear to face Rama's disappointment. The best thing for me would be to end my life here. Some of you may go back and report the truth."

One of the leaders of the party was an experienced devotee and elder of the name of Jambavan, who although now in the form of a bear was a ripe soul full of knowledge and wisdom. He said to Angada, "You are your mother's only hope and the anointed heir-apparent, and it is your duty to live. You must go back and tell Rama the truth that you have not discovered Sita's whereabouts; and he will perhaps tell you what you should do next, and you may also tell him all the others you have left behind here have ended their lives."

At this moment Hanuman said, "We have, of course, exceeded the time given to us, but that is unimportant. Do you realize that there are many other parts of this world and other worlds where we may have to search? Do not despair or give up. There is much that we could still do. If we are to die let us die in a battle. Remember Jatayu, how he died nobly fighting Ravana to the last."

This sounded very encouraging in the present gloom, and the mention of Jatayu brought an unexpected repercussion. When his name was mentioned, they suddenly saw a new creature approaching them. Unidentifiable and gigantic, it approached their group with difficulty but with resolute strength. At the sight of this grotesque being, the monkeys withdrew in terror and revulsion. They thought this was a rakshasa in a strange guise. Hanuman stood up to face it and said challengingly, "Whether you are an asura or Ravana himself in this form, do not hope to escape me. I will destroy you." Whereupon it shed tears and begged, "Tell me all about Jatayu." Hanuman said, "Tell me who you are first and then I will explain, and the other said, "My name is Sampathi and I am the elder brother of Jatayu. Long ago, we were separated and now I heard you mention his death. Is he dead? Who killed him and why?"

Hanuman spent time consoling the grief-stricken Sampathi, who then told his story: "We were both sons of Aruna, the charioteer of the sun god. We were very happy, skimming and floating in the higher skies. One day we decided to fly higher than ever so that we might have a glimpse of the heavens where the gods reside. We flew together higher and higher and crossed the path of the sun god, who felt irritated at the sight of us, and when he turned his full energy in our direction, Jatayu, who was protected in the shadow of my wings, was unhurt; but my feathers and wings were all burnt and charred and I fell as a heap of bones and flesh on this mountain. It has all along been a life of great suffering for me and I have survived because of the help of a sage who lives in this mountain. I have had enough determination to survive because I was told my redemption would come when I heard the name of Rama uttered within my earshot."

When he said this, Hanuman and his men cried in one voice, "Victory to Rama!" At this the creature underwent a transformation: his feathers grew again and his wings became large enough to lift him in the skies, and he developed into a most majestic bird. When he found that Hanuman and his followers were in despair about finding Sita, he said, "Ravana went this way with Sita. I saw him carrying Sita off to Lanka, which is farther south, and he has imprisoned her there. You will have to cross the sea somehow, and find out her whereabouts. Do not be disheartened by this expanse of water before you. You will ultimately succeed in your mission. Now I must take leave of you; our tribe is without a leader since Jatayu is dead. I must take on his duties." Saying this, Sampathi floated up and flew away.

After Sampathi left, they conferred among themselves as to how the sea was to be crossed, which they felt an utterly hopeless task to attempt, until Jambavan spoke once again. He said to Hanuman, "You are the only one who is fit to cross the sea and carry the message of hope to Sita." He explained, "You are unaware of your own stature. That is a part of a curse laid on you long ago by your father—that you should be ignorant of both the depths of your learning and your own powers. This delusion will have to be overcome before you attempt anything further now. Remember that you can grow to any stature you wish and if you so decide, you can cover the entire world in one stride, outdoing even Vishnu in the days of Mahabali. Make yourself as immense as you need and you can have one foot on this shore and another across the sea, on the other shore—that will be Lanka. When you have reached Lanka, make yourself inconspicuous and your devotion to Rama will be enough to guide you to where Sita is kept."

Hanuman listened to this with his head bowed in humility. "Your words give me so much courage that I feel I can vanquish and eradicate the entire race of asuras if they will not yield to me my Goddess Mother. The span of this ocean seems to me insignificant. The grace you have conferred on me and Rama's command are like two wings which will carry me anywhere." So saying he assumed a gigantic stature; the mountain called Mahendra, which had till then loomed high up in the clouds, now seemed like a pebble at his feet. He stood there looking southward choosing his own moment to step across the ocean into Lanka.

8

MEMENTO FROM RAMA

Landing on the soil of Lanka, Hanuman shrank himself to an unnoticeable size and began his search for Sita. He peeped into every building in the city. He saw several streets with houses in which Ravana had kept his collection of women from several parts of this world and other worlds. Since Ravana had grown indifferent to them after his infatuation with Sita, he ignored his favourites completely and Hanuman noticed that in every house, women sat longingly, hoping for Ravana's return to their embraces. Hanuman presently came into an elaborate mansion with rich furnishings where he saw a woman of great beauty lolling in her bed while several attendants were fanning her.

"Here is the end of my quest," Hanuman said to himself, thinking that it might be Sita; he studied her features closely, recollecting again and again the description given to him by Rama. He was filled with pain and anger at the thought that Rama's wife was living in such luxury, perhaps after yielding herself to Ravana. He almost wept at the thought that while Rama was undergoing such suffering in his quest for his wife, she should live in luxury now. For a moment, Hanuman felt that there was nothing more for him to do, and that all his plans to help Rama had come to an abrupt end.

While he sat there on the roof unobtrusively watching, he realized he might be mistaken. Observing her further, he noticed several differences in the features of this woman. In spite of her beauty she had a touch of coarseness. She slept inelegantly with her arms and legs clumsily flung about, with her lips parted; she snored; and she talked in her sleep incoherently. "No, this could be anyone but the goddess I am seeking," Hanuman told himself with relief; and presently he understood that this was Ravana's wife, Mandodari.

Hanuman next moved on into Ravana's palace, observed him in his luxurious setting and, after satisfying himself that Sita was not imprisoned there, passed on. After exhausting his search of all the buildings he decided to search the woods and gardens. He finally arrived at Asoka Vana. It was Ravana's favourite retreat, a magnificent park land with orchards and grottoes and pleasure gardens. When Hanuman came atop a simsupa tree, he observed several rakshasa women, grotesque looking and fierce, armed with weapons, sleeping on the ground. Sita was seated in their midst. He studied her closely: she answered all points of the description given by Rama. Now Hanuman's doubts were gone; but it rent his heart to see her in her present state, unkempt, undecorated, with a single piece of yellow sari covering her body, and with the dust of many days on her. Suddenly the rakshasa women got up from their sleep, closed in on Sita, and menaced and frightened her. Sita shrank away from them, but challenged them to do their worst.

Presently the tormentors saw Ravana arriving and drew aside. He approached Sita with endearing words. He alternated between frightening and cajoling her into becoming his prime mistress. But she spurned all his advances. Hanuman shuddered at the spectacle before him but was also filled with profound respect and admiration for Sita.

Eventually Ravana went off in a great rage, ordering the fierce women to be unrelenting and break her will. After he left, the women became so menacing that Sita cried, "O Rama! Have you forgotten me?" Presently the women retired and Sita made preparations to end her life by hanging herself from a nearby tree. At this moment, Hanuman slowly appeared before Sita, fearful lest he startle her, and hurriedly narrated who he was and why he was there. He explained all that had happened these many months; he answered all her doubts and established his identity. Finally he showed her Rama's ring. His assurances and his message proved a turning point in Sita's life. She gave him a single piece of jewellery that she had saved (concealed in a knot at her sari-end), and requested him to deliver it to Rama as her memento.

Before he left, Hanuman assumed an enormous stature, destroyed the Asoka Vana, and damaged many parts of Lanka, so as to make his visit noticed. When news of this depredation reached Ravana, he dispatched a regular army to attack and capture this monkey, but it eluded them. Finally Ravana sent his son Indrajit, who caught and bound the monkey (for Hanuman allowed this to happen) and took him captive to the court. Ravana questioned who he was and who had sent him to destroy this land. Hanuman utilized this opportunity to speak about Rama, advise Ravana to change his ways, and warn him of imminent destruction at Rama's hands.

Ravana in great fury ordered him to be destroyed; but his brother Vibishana interceded, reminding him that it would be improper to kill a messenger, and saved Hanuman. Whereupon Ravana had his tail padded with cotton soaked in oil and set it on fire. Hanuman extricated himself from his bonds and ran over the rooftops of all the mansions and other buildings, setting fire to Ravana's splendid capital. After satisfying himself that he had reduced it to ashes (leaving the tree under which Sita sat untouched), he hastened back to Rama's camp and reported to him fully all that he had seen and done.

9

RAVANA IN COUNCIL

Ravana's capital, after its destruction by Hanuman, was rebuilt by the divine architect Maya. Surveying it now, Ravana forgot for a moment the setback he had suffered, and was lost in admiration of the work of the architect. He entered his new council hall surrounded by his relations and admirers; but after a while he ordered everyone out except his brothers and army chiefs and conferred with them behind closed doors. From his royal seat, he said, "At this moment, let us not forget that my authority has been challenged not by a warrior but by a monkey! What were our army chiefs so resplendently decorated doing when this ludicrous situation was developing? In our wells, instead of water rising from the springs, there is blood. The smoke in the air is not from sacrificial fires but from the smouldering ruins of mansions and homes. The scent in the air is not of rare incense but of burnt nails and hair. I have lost many a friend and relative, not to speak of subjects, and all this has been accomplished by a monkey! Now let us consider what we should do next. We do not have even the satisfaction of saying that we have caught the monkey and destroyed it! I want you, all the great men assembled here, to advise me frankly and speak out your minds."

Whereupon his commander-in-chief said, "Abducting a woman when her husband is away is not the work of a hero. Those two human beings, Rama and his brother, have wiped out such warriors as Kara and fourteen thousand troops under his command; and they have mutilated your sister. You should have dealt first with the men and then taken the woman. That would have been the simplest solution. You ignored everything and took that woman in haste and now lament that your authority is shaken. Or even later, instead of sitting back and enjoying the life of this beautiful city, you should have ordered us to go out and kill those two on their own ground. You did not do that. Now we must go forth, search out those who have inspired this monkey, and finish them. If we do not accomplish it in time, what has begun with a monkey may not end with a monkey. Next even a swarm of mosquitoes may decide to challenge your authority. We must act; this is no time for brooding on the past."

When he sat down, the next one, called Mahodara, a giant among giants, rose and said, "Chief! Before your might which has shaken Mount Kailas and brought all the great gods as supplicants at your feet, a monkey's pranks should be ignored. Permit me. I will go and drink the blood of those who have set this monkey on us and come back within a trice."

Another one got up and said, "After all, monkeys and human beings are created by Brahma for our food. It is not beyond our power to cross this little ocean and put an end to their activities. Why give this so much thought? Could one ever be afraid of one's food?" Others got up, practically repeating what had been said by the previous speakers, and emphasizing the greatness of Ravana and the meanness of their enemies. They worked themselves into a mood of such contempt that they came to the conclusion, "To go after a couple of human beings heading a horde of monkeys, with all the paraphernalia of war, would not be in keeping with our dignity. We should rather wait for the creatures to venture onto our soil, in their own time, and then we can end their adventure."

Then Kumbakarna, Ravana's brother, rose to say a few plain words. "You have done incompatible things. You have desired to appropriate another man's wife, which is against all codes of conduct, and now you are thinking of your prestige, reputation, status, fame, might, and eminence. My dear brother, you snatched away a beautiful woman, turning a deaf ear to her screams and appeals, and have kept her in prison all these months. And this has brought us the present catastrophe. But now consider deeply. Do you want to restore her to her husband

and seek peace or not? Since you have gone so far, you should keep her and let us fight for her possession. And if we are victorious, well and good, but if we die, let us die. My dear brother, I am now ready to lead an army against our enemies. Let us not delay."

Ravana said, "My boy, you have spoken truly what I feel at heart. Let us raise our flags, gather our armies and march forward immediately."

Now Ravana's son, Indrajit, said, "Great one! You should not bestir yourself in this manner. After all, we are not being opposed by a regular infantry, cavalry, or elephants, but by a crowd of monkeys and some men. You should not trouble yourself to meet them. Leave it to me. I will let go my arrows, and you will find the shrunken-faced monkeys chattering and running away. And then I will go and, I promise you, bring the heads of Rama and Lakshmana and place them at your feet. Stay where you are."

When he said this, Vibishana, Ravana's youngest brother, interrupted the young man. "You do not know what you are saying." He addressed Ravana: "I speak in sorrow. You are everything to me: a father, leader, and guru. What grieves me is that you are about to lose the position which you have attained through so much effort. I speak from my heart, with sincerity, and after much deliberation; I cannot shout like others and I have not the daring to speak challengingly. But I am speaking what I feel is the truth. Please listen to me fully without losing your patience. What really set this city on fire was not the torch at a monkey's tail, but the flame that rages in the soul of a woman called Janaki. A man loses his honour and name only through lust and avarice. You have acquired extraordinary powers through your own spiritual performances but you have misused your powers and attacked the very gods that gave you the power, and now you pursue evil ways. Is there anyone who has conquered the gods and lived continuously in that victory? Sooner or later retribution has always come. Do not be contemptuous of men or monkeys. Remember that you have never asked for protection from human beings; remember also that Nandi cursed you when you lifted the Kailas mountain, saying that your end would come through a monkey; and later when you attempted to molest Vedavathi, seizing her by the hair, did she not curse you before jumping into fire, saying that one day she would be reborn and be responsible for the end of your island as well as your life?

"If you look deeply into the signs of the times, perhaps all these three curses are working out. But maybe you could still avoid disaster. Remember that as long as you keep Sita a prisoner, you and your subjects will have no peace. Think of Rama's heritage, Dasaratha's achievements, and all the other glorious deeds of the members of the Ikshvahu race. They are not ordinary men nor are the monkeys supporting them mere monkeys. The gods have assumed that form, only because you have had immunity from the gods conferred on you. Now a word more. Release the goddess you have imprisoned. And that will prove to be the most meritorious achievement of your career."

Ravana glared at his brother and said with a bitter laugh, "You began with agreeable sentences and sentiments but you go on prattling away like a madman. Is it out of fear or out of love for those human beings? You remind me that I have not asked for protection from human beings. Does one have to ask for such a thing? Did I ever ask for the blessing of being able to lift Kailas? You speak without any thought. You think I have conquered the gods because of the boon conferred on me by them. I do not have to wait for anybody's boon to do what I please. Nobody's curse can ever touch me.

"Why are you lost in such admiration for Rama? Because he snapped the old rusty bow of Shiva? Or sent his arrows through the trunks of those seven decaying trees? Lost his kingdom because of a hunchbacked woman? Killed Vali without daring to come up before him? Lost his wife through a very simple trick that I tried? I am astonished that after all this he has not taken his own life but continues to breathe and move about! And indeed you are his admirer! You think that he is likely to be an incarnation of Vishnu. What if he is? I am not afraid of Vishnu or anybody. Particularly Vishnu, who has been the most defeated god, having never won a single battle."

After saying this, Ravana cried, "Let us now go forth for battle." He looked at Vibishana and said, "Let those who like, come with me."

Vibishana made one more attempt to stop him. "Don't go," he pleaded.

"Is it because he is Vishnu?" Ravana asked contemptuously. "Where was he when I imprisoned Indra, and destroyed his mighty elephants by plucking their ivory tusks out of their heads? Was this God a baby then? When I seized the three worlds, defeating even Shiva and Brahma, where was this God of yours? In hiding? Did this God abandon his gigantic universal form and reduce himself to human size in order to make it easier for us to swallow him? Don't follow me if you are afraid, but stay in this vast city, which is spacious and comfortable. Don't disturb yourself," Ravana said and, clapping his hands, laughed uproariously.

Still, next day Vibishana visited him privately and tried to hold him back with further arguments. This infuriated Ravana. "You hate our own kinsmen and you have begun to admire and love Rama and Lakshmana. At the thought of them, your eyes are filled with tears, and you melt to the bone in tender feeling. You want to gain the friendship of my avowed enemy. I suspect you have planned your future with deep thought. You are treacherous. I remember now that when that monkey was brought before me and I ordered him to be destroyed and eaten by our servants, you interceded, saying that we should not kill an emissary. I now realize that you were carried away by the rantings of that monkey when he sang the praise of his master and narrated his achievements. You simpleton! You wanted this country to be destroyed by fire, I know. You have your deep-laid plans, I know. I should not live any more with this poison called my younger brother. Now leave me. If I do not kill you, it is because I do not want to earn the odium of murdering a younger brother, but if you persist in staying before me, you will die by my hand."

When he heard this, Vibishana withdrew with four others, but before parting he said, "It is your misfortune that you are swayed by the words of mean minds and are deaf to justice and fair play. I fear that your entire race is going to be annihilated.

I will now go away as you order. I tried to tell you what seems befitting. You are still my leader and chief but I leave you. Forgive my mistakes or if I have hurt your feelings."

So saying, Vibishana crossed the seas and reached Rama's camp on the other shore, where the monkey armies were gathered in an enormous array.

10

ACROSS THE OCEAN

As Vibishana noticed Rama standing at the edge of the sea, brooding, perhaps, on plans to rescue Sita, he kept himself in the background, not wishing to break in on him at just that moment. Later, however, when the chiefs of Rama's army noticed his presence, they took him to be a spy and treated him roughly. At this Vibishana cried aloud, "O Rama! I am here to seek asylum. I seek your grace and protection."

When the cry reached Rama, he dispatched messengers to fetch the supplicant before him. Hanuman also sent a special messenger, to protect the visitor (whom the monkey army thought was Ravana himself, in disguise, delivered into their hands) and to investigate his antecedents. The messenger questioned Vibishana and reported back to Rama. Rama thought it over and asked his battle companions one by one what they thought of the visitor.

Sugreeva said, "One who has behaved traitorously to his brother—how can we trust him? I was no friend of my brother, but my case was different. I was chased for my life, deprived of my wife, and Vali left me no choice. But in this case, by his own admission, his brother Ravana was kind, but still he has snapped his ties and come here. It looks to me very strange indeed. We cannot admit him in our camp. After all, you are on a mission to wipe out the asura class; and in spite of all his noble speech, this person is really an asura."

Then Jambavan came forward to say, "We take a risk when we admit anyone from an enemy's camp; and it will be too late when you discover the fact. Asuras are well known for their trickeries and disguises. Remember that what appeared to be a golden deer turned out to be Mareecha."

Rama lent a patient hearing to everyone and asked his commander-in-chief to speak. He said, "I have some knowledge of what the books have to say regarding agents, spies, and refugees. Only those who have suffered treachery in the hands of the enemy, or an enemy's soldier who turns his back, unable to fight any more, or an enemy's neighbour who has lost his home and family—when these come, even if they happen to be the kinsmen of your worst enemy, you can admit them and accept their friendship. If we consider Vibishana's case and analyse the time of his arrival and the circumstances, nothing was done to drive him hither. How can we trust his mere profession of virtue and goodness? We cannot fit him into any of the categories of refugees defined in our shastras." Many others spoke, and unanimously declared that Vibishana should be rejected.

Rama looked at Hanuman and said, "You have not said anything. What do you think?"

Hanuman said, "When all your advisers have spoken so very clearly I hesitate to express my thoughts, but since you give me the privilege, let me assure you that I do not think this man is evil-minded. Looking at him, it is very clear to me that he has a clean and pure soul and that his heart is good. I am sure he has come to you through devotion. I have every reason to think he has come with a sense of adoration for you. He has heard of your help to Sugreeva, he has heard of your surrender to Bharatha, he knows your mind and has come to you because he feels convinced that you could help him, and save him from the tyranny of his brother. He did his best to save his brother but failed. When I went to Lanka and looked about, I had occasion to look into his home; unlike the homes of others of his family, which are filled with meat and wine and women, his home is that of a man of piety and purity. When Ravana ordered that I should be killed, it was Vibishana who interceded and persuaded him to spare my life as I was only an emissary. At that time he had no intention of coming over here and so it was not a calculated step. He is genuine, and he seeks your protection. We should accept him without further thought."

After listening to Hanuman, Rama declared, "I agree with you. After all, one who seeks asylum must be given protection. Whatever may happen later, it is our first duty to protect. Even if I am defeated because I have taken him at his word, I would not mind it; I shall still have done the right thing. On the other hand, if I am victorious in war by rejecting him, to me that victory would not be worth having. One who speaks for himself must be accepted at his face value. One who seeks asylum must be protected. One of my ancestors gave his life to protect a dove which sought his protection from a hawk. I have made up my mind and my friends here please take note of it. Let him be brought in." He looked at Sugreeva and said, "You should go and tell him that we accept him. Welcome him and bring him here."

Very soon Sugreeva led Vibishana to Rama's presence. Rama spoke kind words to him. Vibishana accepted Rama's friendship with grace and humility. Finally Rama turned to Lakshmana and said, "Treat Vibishana as a ruler of Lanka, but now in exile, and give him all the comforts he needs and all the honours worthy of a king."

Vibishana explained, "It was not my purpose to seek the crown of Lanka, but since you confer it on me, I have to accept it. Believe me, sir, my only purpose in coming here was to be with you and receive your grace." Day by day they conferred, and Vibishana explained the disposition of Ravana's troops, the nature of his weapons, and the strength of his army, all of which enabled Rama to draw up a precise plan of attack on Lanka.

Rama's next phase of operation was to try and cross the seas. He stood on the shore of the ocean and the more he looked at it, the more desperate he felt as to how he was to cross it with his army. He prayed and fasted for seven days and summoned the sea god and ordered, "Make way for my armies."

The sea god said, "I am as much subject to the laws of nature as other elements. What can I do?"

Whereupon Rama felt angry and threatened to shoot his arrows into the sea so that all the water might evaporate and facilitate his passage. The sea god implored him to desist and not to destroy the sea and its living creatures, and suggested, "I will accept and put to the best use whatever is brought to me to bridge the sea."

Rama's angry mood left him and he said, "So be it." Very soon his monkey army brought in mud, huge rocks, and even pieces of mountains; men, monkeys, and all animals helped in this task. It was said that even the little squirrel rolled along pebbles to fill up the sea, and a day came when there was a passage created by their combined efforts, and Rama's army marched across and landed on the soil of Lanka.

I I
THE SIEGE OF LANKA*

Ravana deployed the pick of his divisions to guard the approaches to the capital and appointed his trusted generals and kinsmen in special charge of key places. Gradually, however, his world began to shrink. As the fight developed he lost his associates one by one. No one who went out returned.

He tried some devious measures in desperation. He sent spies in the garb of Rama's monkey army across to deflect and corrupt some of Rama's staunchest supporters, such as Sugreeva, on whom rested the entire burden of this war. He employed sorcerers to disturb the mind of Sita, hoping that if she yielded, Rama would ultimately lose heart. He ordered a sorcerer to create a decapitated head resembling Rama's and placed it before Sita as evidence of Rama's defeat. Sita, although shaken at first, very soon recovered her composure and remained unaffected by the spectacle.

At length a messenger from Rama arrived, saying, "Rama bids me warn you that your doom is at hand. Even now it is not too late for you to restore Sita and beg Rama's forgiveness. You have troubled the world too long. You are not fit to continue as King. At our camp, your brother, Vibishana, has already been crowned the King of this land, and the world knows all people will be happy under him."

Ravana ordered the messenger to be killed instantly. But it was more easily said than done, the messenger being Angada, the son of mighty Vali. When two rakshasas came to seize him, he tucked one of them under each arm, rose into the sky, and

*From Gods, Demons, and Others.

flung the rakshasas down. In addition, he kicked and broke off the tower of Ravana's palace, and left. Ravana viewed the broken tower with dismay.

Rama awaited the return of Angada, and, on hearing his report, decided that there was no further cause to hope for a change of heart in Ravana and immediately ordered the assault on Lanka.

As the fury of the battle grew, both sides lost sight of the distinction between night and day. The air was filled with the cries of fighters, their challenges, cheers, and imprecations; buildings and trees were torn up and, as one of his spies reported to Ravana, the monkeys were like a sea overrunning Lanka. The end did not seem to be in sight.

At one stage of the battle, Rama and Lakshmana were attacked by Indrajit, and the serpent darts employed by him made them swoon on the battlefield. Indrajit went back to his father to proclaim that it was all over with Rama and Lakshmana and soon, without a leader, the monkeys would be annihilated.

Ravana rejoiced to hear it and cried, "Did not I say so? All you fools believed that I should surrender." He added, "Go and tell Sita that Rama and his brother are no more. Take her high up in Pushpak Vimana, my chariot, and show her their bodies on the battlefield." His words were obeyed instantly. Sita, happy to have a chance to glimpse a long-lost face, accepted the chance, went high up, and saw her husband lying dead in the field below. She broke down. "How I wish I had been left alone and not brought up to see this spectacle. Ah, me . . . Help me to put an end to my life."

Trijata, one of Ravana's women, whispered to her, "Don't lose heart, they are not dead," and she explained why they were in a faint.

In due course, the effect of the serpent darts was neutralized when Garuda, the mighty eagle, the born enemy of all serpents, appeared on the scene; the venomous darts enveloping Rama and Lakshmana scattered at the approach of Garuda and the brothers were on their feet again.

From his palace retreat Ravana was surprised to hear again the cheers of the enemy hordes outside the ramparts; the siege was on again. Ravana still had about him his commander-in-chief, his son Indrajit, and five or six others on whom he felt he could rely at the last instance. He sent them one by one. He felt shattered when news came of the death of his commander-in-chief.

"No time to sit back. I will myself go and destroy this Rama and his horde of monkeys," he said and got into his chariot and entered the field.

At this encounter Lakshmana fell down in a faint, and Hanuman hoisted Rama on his shoulders and charged in the direction of Ravana. The main combatants were face to face for the first time. At the end of this engagement Ravana was sorely wounded, his crown was shattered, and his chariot was broken. Helplessly, bare-handed, he stood before Rama, and Rama said, "You may go now and come back tomorrow with fresh weapons." For the first time in his existence of many thousand years, Ravana faced the humiliation of accepting a concession, and he returned crestfallen to his palace.

He ordered that his brother Kumbakarna, famous for his deep sleep, should be awakened. He could depend upon him, and only on him now. It was a mighty task to wake up Kumbakarna. A small army had to be engaged. They sounded trumpets and drums at his ears and were ready with enormous quantities of food and drink for him, for when Kumbakarna awoke from sleep, his hunger was phenomenal and he made a meal of whomever he could grab at his bedside. They cudgelled, belaboured, pushed, pulled, and shook him, with the help of elephants; at last he opened his eyes and swept his arms about and crushed quite a number among those who had stirred him up. When he had eaten and drunk, he was approached by Ravana's chief minister and told, "My lord, the battle is going badly for us."

"Which battle?" he asked, not yet fully awake.

And they had to refresh his memory. "Your brother has fought and has been worsted; our enemies are breaking in, our fort walls are crumbling. . . ."

Kumbakarna was roused. "Why did not anyone tell me all this before? Well, it is not too late; I will deal with that Rama.

His end is come." Thus saying, he strode into Ravana's chamber and said, "Don't worry about anything any more. I will take care of everything."

Ravana spoke with anxiety and defeat in his voice. Kumbakarna, who had never seen him in this state, said, "You have gone on without heeding anyone's words and brought yourself to this pass. You should have fought Rama and acquired Sita. You were led away by mere lust and never cared for anyone's words. . . . Hm . . . This is no time to speak of dead events. I will not forsake you as others have done. I'll bring Rama's head on a platter."

Kumbakarna's entry into the battle created havoc. He destroyed and swallowed hundreds and thousands of the monkey warriors and came very near finishing off the great Sugreeva himself. Rama himself had to take a hand at destroying this demon; he sent the sharpest of his arrows, which cut Kumbakarna limb from limb; but he fought fiercely with only inches of his body remaining intact. Finally Rama severed his head with an arrow. That was the end of Kumbakarna.

When he heard of it, Ravana lamented, "My right hand is cut off."

One of his sons reminded him, "Why should you despair? You have Brahma's gift of invincibility. You should not grieve." Indrajit told him, "What have you to fear when I am alive?"

Indrajit had the power to remain invisible and fight, and accounted for much destruction in the invader's camp. He also created a figure resembling Sita, carried her in his chariot, took her before Rama's army and killed her within their sight.

This completely demoralized the monkeys, who suspended their fight, crying, "Why should we fight when our goddess Sita is thus gone?" They were in a rout until Vibishana came to their rescue and rallied them again.

Indrajit fell by Lakshmana's hand in the end. When he heard of his son's death, Ravana shed bitter tears and swore, "This is the time to kill that woman Sita, the cause of all this misery."

A few encouraged this idea, but one of his councillors advised, "Don't defeat your own purpose and integrity by killing a woman. Let your anger scorch Rama and his brother. Gather all your armies and go and vanquish Rama and Lakshmana, you know you can, and then take Sita. Put on your blessed armour and go forth."

RAMA AND RAVANA
IN BATTLE

Every moment, news came to Ravana of fresh disasters in his camp. One by one, most of his commanders were lost. No one who went forth with battle cries was heard of again. Cries and shouts and the wailings of the widows of warriors came over the chants and songs of triumph that his courtiers arranged to keep up at a loud pitch in his assembly hall. Ravana became restless and abruptly left the hall and went up on a tower, from which he could obtain a full view of the city. He surveyed the scene below but could not stand it. One who had spent a lifetime in destruction, now found the gory spectacle intolerable. Groans and wailings reached his ears with deadly clarity; and he noticed how the monkey hordes revelled in their bloody handiwork. This was too much for him. He felt a terrific rage rising within him, mixed with some admiration for Rama's valour. He told himself, "The time has come for me to act by myself again."

He hurried down the steps of the tower, returned to his chamber, and prepared himself for the battle. He had a ritual bath and performed special prayers to gain the benediction of Shiva; donned his battle dress, matchless armour, armlets, and crowns. He had on a protective armour for every inch of his body. He girt his sword-belt and attached to his body his accoutrements for protection and decoration.

When he emerged from his chamber, his heroic appearance was breathtaking. He summoned his chariot, which could be drawn by horses or move on its own if the horses were hurt or killed. People stood aside when he came out of the palace and entered his chariot. "This is my resolve," he said to himself:

"Either that woman Sita, or my wife Mandodari, will soon have cause to cry and roll in the dust in grief. Surely, before this day is done, one of them will be a widow."

The gods in heaven noticed Ravana's determined move and felt that Rama would need all the support they could muster. They requested Indra to send down his special chariot for Rama's use. When the chariot appeared at his camp, Rama was deeply impressed with the magnitude and brilliance of the vehicle. "How has this come to be here?" he asked.

"Sir," the charioteer answered, "my name is Matali. I have the honour of being the charioteer of Indra. Brahma, the four-faced god and the creator of the Universe, and Shiva, whose power has emboldened Ravana now to challenge you, have commanded me to bring it here for your use. It can fly swifter than air over all obstacles, over any mountain, sea, or sky, and will help you to emerge victorious in this battle."

Rama reflected aloud, "It may be that the rakshasas have created this illusion for me. It may be a trap. I don't know how to view it." Whereupon Matali spoke convincingly to dispel the doubt in Rama's mind. Rama, still hesitant, though partially convinced, looked at Hanuman and Lakshmana and asked, "What do you think of it?" Both answered, "We feel no doubt that this chariot is Indra's; it is not an illusory creation."

Rama fastened his sword, slung two quivers full of rare arrows over his shoulders, and climbed into the chariot.

The beat of war drums, the challenging cries of soldiers, the trumpets, and the rolling chariots speeding along to confront each other, created a deafening mixture of noise. While Ravana had instructed his charioteer to speed ahead, Rama very gently ordered his chariot-driver, "Ravana is in a rage; let him perform all the antics he desires and exhaust himself. Until then be calm; we don't have to hurry forward. Move slowly and calmly, and you must strictly follow my instructions; I will tell you when to drive faster."

Ravana's assistant and one of his staunchest supporters, Mahodara—the giant among giants in his physical appearance— begged Ravana, "Let me not be a mere spectator when you confront Rama. Let me have the honour of grappling with him. Permit me to attack Rama."

"Rama is my sole concern," Ravana replied. "If you wish to engage yourself in a fight, you may fight his brother Lakshmana."

Noticing Mahodara's purpose, Rama steered his chariot across his path in order to prevent Mahodara from reaching Lakshmana. Whereupon Mahodara ordered his chariot-driver, "Now dash straight ahead, directly into Rama's chariot."

The charioteer, more practical-minded, advised him, "I would not go near Rama. Let us keep away." But Mahodara, obstinate and intoxicated with war fever, made straight for Rama. He wanted to have the honour of a direct encounter with Rama himself in spite of Ravana's advice; and for this honour he paid a heavy price, as it was a moment's work for Rama to destroy him, and leave him lifeless and shapeless on the field. Noticing this, Ravana's anger mounted further. He commanded his driver, "You will not slacken now. Go." Many ominous signs were seen now—his bow-strings suddenly snapped; the mountains shook; thunders rumbled in the skies; tears flowed from the horses' eyes; elephants with decorated foreheads moved along dejectedly. Ravana, noticing them, hesitated only for a second, saying, "I don't care. This mere mortal Rama is of no account, and these omens do not concern me at all." Meanwhile, Rama paused for a moment to consider his next step; and suddenly turned towards the armies supporting Ravana, which stretched away to the horizon, and destroyed them. He felt that this might be one way of saving Ravana. With his armies gone, it was possible that Ravana might have a change of heart. But it had only the effect of spurring Ravana on; he plunged forward and kept coming nearer Rama and his own doom.

Rama's army cleared and made way for Ravana's chariot, unable to stand the force of his approach. Ravana blew his conch and its shrill challenge reverberated through space. Following it another conch, called "Panchajanya," which belonged to Mahavishnu (Rama's original form before his present incarnation), sounded of its own accord in answer to the challenge, agitating the universe with its vibrations. And then Matali picked up

another conch, which was Indra's, and blew it. This was the sig-
nal indicating the commencement of the actual battle. Presently
Ravana sent a shower of arrows on Rama; and Rama's follow-
ers, unable to bear the sight of his body being studded with ar-
rows, averted their heads. Then the chariot horses of Ravana
and Rama glared at each other in hostility, and the flags topping
the chariots—Ravana's ensign of the Veena and Rama's with the
whole universe on it—clashed, and one heard the stringing and
twanging of bow-strings on both sides, overpowering in volume
all other sound. Then followed a shower of arrows from Rama's
own bow. Ravana stood gazing at the chariot sent by Indra and
swore, "These gods, instead of supporting me, have gone to the
support of this petty human being. I will teach them a lesson.
He is not fit to be killed with my arrows but I shall seize him and
his chariot together and fling them into high heaven and dash
them to destruction." Despite his oath, he still strung his bow
and sent a shower of arrows at Rama, raining in thousands, but
they were all invariably shattered and neutralized by the arrows
from Rama's bow, which met arrow for arrow. Ultimately Ra-
vana, instead of using one bow, used ten with his twenty arms,
multiplying his attack tenfold; but Rama stood unhurt.

Ravana suddenly realized that he should change his tactics
and ordered his charioteer to fly the chariot up in the skies.
From there he attacked and destroyed a great many of the mon-
key army supporting Rama. Rama ordered Matali, "Go up in
the air. Our young soldiers are being attacked from the sky.
Follow Ravana, and don't slacken."

There followed an aerial pursuit at dizzying speed across the
dome of the sky and rim of the earth. Ravana's arrows came
down like rain; he was bent upon destroying everything in the
world. But Rama's arrows diverted, broke, or neutralized Ra-
vana's. Terror-stricken, the gods watched this pursuit. Presently
Ravana's arrows struck Rama's horses and pierced the heart of
Matali himself. The charioteer fell. Rama paused for a while in
grief, undecided as to his next step. Then he recovered and re-
sumed his offensive. At that moment the divine eagle Garuda
was seen perched on Rama's flagpost, and the gods who were
watching felt that this could be an auspicious sign.

After circling the globe several times, the duelling chariots returned, and the fight continued over Lanka. It was impossible to be very clear about the location of the battleground as the fight occurred here, there, and everywhere. Rama's arrows pierced Ravana's armour and made him wince. Ravana was so insensible to pain and impervious to attack that for him to wince was a good sign, and the gods hoped that this was a turn for the better. But at this moment, Ravana suddenly changed his tactics. Instead of merely shooting his arrows, which were powerful in themselves, he also invoked several supernatural forces to create strange effects: He was an adept in the use of various asthras which could be made dynamic with special incantations. At this point, the fight became one of attack with supernatural powers, and parrying of such an attack with other supernatural powers.

Ravana realized that the mere aiming of shafts with ten or twenty of his arms would be of no avail because the mortal whom he had so contemptuously thought of destroying with a slight effort was proving formidable, and his arrows were beginning to pierce and cause pain. Among the asthras sent by Ravana was one called "Danda," a special gift from Shiva, capable of pursuing and pulverizing its target. When it came flaming along, the gods were struck with fear. But Rama's arrow neutralized it.

Now Ravana said to himself, "These are all petty weapons. I should really get down to proper business." And he invoked the one called "Maya"—a weapon which created illusions and confused the enemy.

With proper incantations and worship, he sent off this weapon and it created an illusion of reviving all the armies and its leaders—Kumbakarna and Indrajit and the others—and bringing them back to the battlefield. Presently Rama found all those who, he thought, were no more, coming on with battle cries and surrounding him. Every man in the enemy's army was again up in arms. They seemed to fall on Rama with victorious cries. This was very confusing and Rama asked Matali, whom he had by now revived, "What is happening now? How are all these coming back? They were dead." Matali explained, "In your original identity you are the creator of illusions in this universe. Please know that Ravana has created phantoms to confuse you. If you make up your mind, you can dispel them immediately." Matali's explanation was a great help. Rama at once invoked a weapon called "Gnana"—which means "wisdom" or "perception." This was a very rare weapon, and he sent it forth. And all the terrifying armies who seemed to have come on in such a great mass suddenly evaporated into thin air.

Ravana then shot an asthra called "Thama," whose nature was to create total darkness in all the worlds. The arrows came with heads exposing frightening eyes and fangs, and fiery tongues. End to end the earth was enveloped in total darkness and the whole of creation was paralysed. This asthra also created a deluge of rain on one side, a rain of stones on the other, a hail-storm showering down intermittently, and a tornado sweeping the earth. Ravana was sure that this would arrest Rama's enterprise. But Rama was able to meet it with what was named "Shivasthra." He understood the nature of the phenomenon and the cause of it and chose the appropriate asthra for counteracting it.

Ravana now shot off what he considered his deadliest weapon—a trident endowed with extraordinary destructive power, once gifted to Ravana by the gods. When it started on its journey there was real panic all round. It came on flaming toward Rama, its speed or course unaffected by the arrows he flung at it.

When Rama noticed his arrows falling down ineffectively while the trident sailed towards him, for a moment he lost heart. When it came quite near, he uttered a certain mantra from the depth of his being and while he was breathing out that incantation, an esoteric syllable in perfect timing, the trident collapsed. Ravana, who had been so certain of vanquishing Rama with his trident, was astonished to see it fall down within an inch of him, and for a minute wondered if his adversary might not after all be a divine being although he looked like a mortal. Ravana thought to himself, "This is, perhaps, the highest God. Who could he be? Not Shiva, for Shiva is my supporter; he could not be Brahma, who is four faced; could not be

Vishnu, because of my immunity from the weapons of the whole trinity. Perhaps this man is the primordial being, the cause behind the whole universe. But whoever he may be, I will not stop my fight until I defeat and crush him or at least take him prisoner."

With this resolve, Ravana next sent a weapon which issued forth monstrous serpents vomiting fire and venom, with enormous fangs and red eyes. They came darting in from all directions.

Rama now selected an asthra called "Garuda" (which meant "eagle"). Very soon thousands of eagles were aloft, and they picked off the serpents with their claws and beaks and destroyed them. Seeing this also fail, Ravana's anger was roused to a mad pitch and he blindly emptied a quiverful of arrows in Rama's direction. Rama's arrows met them half way and turned them round so that they went back and their sharp points embedded themselves in Ravana's own chest.

Ravana was weakening in spirit. He realized that he was at the end of his resources. All his learning and equipment in weaponry were of no avail and he had practically come to the end of his special gifts of destruction. While he was going down thus, Rama's own spirit was soaring up. The combatants were now near enough to grapple with each other and Rama realized that this was the best moment to cut off Ravana's heads. He sent a crescent-shaped arrow which sliced off one of Ravana's heads and flung it far into the sea, and this process continued; but every time a head was cut off, Ravana had the benediction of having another one grown in its place. Rama's crescent-shaped weapon was continuously busy as Ravana's heads kept cropping up. Rama lopped off his arms but they grew again and every lopped-off arm hit Matali and the chariot and tried to cause destruction by itself, and the tongue in a new head wagged, uttered challenges, and cursed Rama. On the cast-off heads of Ravana devils and minor demons, who had all along been in terror of Ravana and had obeyed and pleased him, executed a dance of death and feasted on the flesh.

Ravana was now desperate. Rama's arrows embedded themselves in a hundred places on his body and weakened him.

Presently he collapsed in a faint on the floor of his chariot. Noticing his state, his charioteer pulled back and drew the chariot aside. Matali whispered to Rama, "This is the time to finish off that demon. He is in a faint. Go on. Go on."

But Rama put away his bow and said, "It is not fair warfare to attack a man who is in a faint. I will wait. Let him recover," and waited.

When Ravana revived, he was angry with his charioteer for withdrawing, and took out his sword, crying, "You have disgraced me. Those who look on will think I have retreated." But his charioteer explained how Rama suspended the fight and forebore to attack when he was in a faint. Somehow, Ravana appreciated his explanation and patted his back and resumed his attacks. Having exhausted his special weapons, in desperation Ravana began to throw on Rama all sorts of things such as staves, cast-iron balls, heavy rocks, and oddments he could lay hands on. None of them touched Rama, but glanced off and fell ineffectually. Rama went on shooting his arrows. There seemed to be no end of this struggle in sight.

Now Rama had to pause to consider what final measure he should take to bring this campaign to an end. After much thought, he decided to use "Brahmasthra," a weapon specially designed by the Creator Brahma on a former occasion, when he had to provide one for Shiva to destroy Tripura, the old monster who assumed the forms of flying mountains and settled down on habitations and cities, seeking to destroy the world. The Brahmasthra was a special gift to be used only when all other means had failed. Now Rama, with prayers and worship, invoked its fullest power and sent it in Ravana's direction, aiming at his heart rather than his head; Ravana being vulnerable at heart. While he had prayed for indestructibility of his several heads and arms, he had forgotten to strengthen his heart, where the Brahmasthra entered and ended his career.

Rama watched him fall headlong from his chariot face down onto the earth, and that was the end of the great campaign. Now one noticed Ravana's face aglow with a new quality. Rama's arrows had burnt off the layers of dross, the anger, conceit, cruelty, lust, and egotism which had encrusted his real self,

and now his personality came through in its pristine
one who was devout and capable of tremendous atta.
His constant meditation on Rama, although as an adversary,
now seemed to bear fruit, as his face shone with serenity and
peace. Rama noticed it from his chariot above and commanded
Matali, "Set me down on the ground." When the chariot de-
scended and came to rest on its wheels, Rama got down and
commanded Matali, "I am grateful for your services to me. You
may now take the chariot back to Indra."

Surrounded by his brother Lakshmana and Hanuman and all
his other war chiefs, Rama approached Ravana's body, and
stood gazing on it. He noted his crowns and jewellery scattered
piecemeal on the ground. The decorations and the extraordi-
nary workmanship of the armour on his chest were blood-
covered. Rama sighed as if to say, "What might he not have
achieved but for the evil stirring within him!"

At this moment, as they readjusted Ravana's blood-stained
body, Rama noticed to his great shock a scar on Ravana's back
and said with a smile, "Perhaps this is not an episode of glory
for me as I seem to have killed an enemy who was turning his
back and retreating. Perhaps I was wrong in shooting the Brah-
masthra into him." He looked so concerned at this supposed
lapse on his part that Vibishana, Ravana's brother, came for-
ward to explain. "What you have achieved is unique. I say so
although it meant the death of my brother."

"But I have attacked a man who had turned his back," Rama
said. "See that scar."

Vibishana explained, "It is an old scar. In ancient days, when
he paraded his strength around the globe, once he tried to at-
tack the divine elephants that guard the four directions. When
he tried to catch them, he was gored in the back by one of the
tuskers and that is the scar you see now; it is not a fresh one
though fresh blood is flowing on it."

Rama accepted the explanation. "Honour him and cherish
his memory so that his spirit may go to heaven, where he has
his place. And now I will leave you to attend to his funeral
arrangements, befitting his grandeur."

I 3

INTERLUDE

To Link Up the Narrative, an Extract from "Valmiki"[*]

After the death of Ravana, Rama sent Hanuman as his emissary
to fetch Sita. Sita was overjoyed. She had been in a state of
mourning all along, completely neglectful of her dress and ap-
pearance, and she immediately rose to go out and meet Rama as
she was. But Hanuman explained that it was Rama's express
wish that she should dress and decorate herself before coming
to his presence.

A large crowd pressed around Rama. When Sita eagerly ar-
rived, after her months of loneliness and suffering, she was re-
ceived by her husband in full view of a vast public. She felt
awkward but accepted this with resignation. But what she
could not understand was why her lord seemed preoccupied
and moody and cold. However, she prostrated herself at his feet,
and then stood a little away from him, sensing some strange bar-
rier between herself and him.

Rama remained brooding for a while and suddenly said,
"My task is done. I have now freed you. I have fulfilled my mis-
sion. All this effort has been not to attain personal satisfaction
for you or me. It was to vindicate the honour of the Ikshvahu
race and to honour our ancestors' codes and values. After all
this, I must tell you that it is not customary to admit back to the
normal married fold a woman who has resided all alone in a
stranger's house. There can be no question of our living to-
gether again. I leave you free to go where you please and to
choose any place to live in. I do not restrict you in any manner."

On hearing this, Sita broke down. "My trials are not ended

*From *Gods, Demons, and Others*.

yet," she cried. "I thought with your victory all our troubles were at an end . . . ! So be it." She beckoned to Lakshmana and ordered, "Light a fire at once, on this very spot."

Lakshmana hesitated and looked at his brother, wondering whether he would countermand the order. But Rama seemed passive and acquiescent. Lakshmana, ever the most unquestioning deputy, gathered faggots and got ready a roaring pyre within a short time. The entire crowd watched the proceedings, stunned by the turn of events. The flames rose to the height of a tree; still Rama made no comment. He watched. Sita approached the fire, prostrated herself before it, and said, "O Agni, great god of fire, be my witness." She jumped into the fire.

From the heart of the flame rose the god of fire, bearing Sita, and presented her to Rama with words of blessing. Rama, now satisfied that he had established his wife's integrity in the presence of the world, welcomed Sita back to his arms.

THE CORONATION

Rama explained that he had to adopt this trial in order to demonstrate Sita's purity beyond a shadow of doubt to the whole world. This seemed a rather strange inconsistency on the part of one who had brought back to life and restored to her husband a person like Ahalya, who had avowedly committed a moral lapse; and then there was Sugreeva's wife, who had been forced to live with Vali, and whom Rama commended as worthy of being taken back by Sugreeva after Vali's death. In Sita's case Ravana, in spite of repeated and desperate attempts, could not approach her. She had remained inviolable. And the fiery quality of her essential being burnt out the god of fire himself, as he had admitted after Sita's ordeal. Under these circumstances, it was very strange that Rama should have spoken harshly as he had done at the first sight of Sita, and subjected her to a dreadful trial.

The gods, who had watched this in suspense, were now profoundly relieved but also had an uneasy feeling that Rama had, perhaps, lost sight of his own identity. Again and again this seemed to happen. Rama displayed the tribulations and the limitations of the human frame and it was necessary from time to time to remind him of his divinity. Now Brahma, the Creator, came forward to speak and addressed Rama thus: "Of the Trinity, I am the Creator. Shiva is the Destroyer and Vishnu is the Protector. All three of us derive our existence from the Supreme God and we are subject to dissolution and rebirth. But the Supreme God who creates us is without a beginning or an end. There is neither birth nor growth nor death for the Supreme God. He is the origin of everything and in him everything is assimilated at the end. That God is yourself, and Sita at your side now is a part of that Divinity. Please remember that this is your real identity and let not the fear and doubts that assail an ordinary mortal ever move you. You are beyond everything; and we are all blessed indeed to be in your presence."

In the high heavens, Shiva encouraged Dasaratha to go down to the earth and meet Rama. He said, "Rama needs your benediction after having carried out your commands, and having gone through so much privation for fourteen years in order to safeguard the integrity of your promises." Dasaratha descended in his true form into the midst of his family. Rama was overjoyed to see him again and prostrated himself at his feet.

Dasaratha said, "This moment is one of supreme joy for me. For the first time in all these years, my heart is lighter. The memory of the evil use that Kaikeyi had made of my promise to her had stuck in my heart like a splinter and had stayed there. Although I had shed my physical body, the pain had remained unmitigated—until this minute. It is now gone. You with Sita are the primordial being and I was indeed blessed to have begotten you as my son. This is a moment of fulfillment for me. I have nothing more to say and I will go back to my world and repose there in eternal peace. But before I go I want you to ask of me something, anything, any wish I could fulfill for you."

Rama said, "Your arrival here is the greatest boon for me, and I have nothing more to seek. All along, my only desire has been to see you again, and that is fulfilled." Dasaratha still insisted that Rama should state a wish that he could grant. Rama said, "If that is so, please find a place in your heart for both Kaikeyi and Bharatha, and take back your vow by which you cut off their blood connection with you. I cannot think of her except as a mother and Bharatha as a brother."

Dasaratha at once replied, "Bharatha is different. He has proved his greatness. Yes, I will accept him. But Kaikeyi—she ruined us all. She prevented your being crowned at the last moment. I can never forgive her."

Rama explained, "It was not her mistake. I committed an unforgivable blunder in straightway accepting the kingship when you offered it, without pausing to consider the consequences.

I should have had more forethought. It was not her mistake."
Rama continued his plea for Kaikeyi so earnestly that Dasaratha
finally acceded to it. A burden was lifted from Rama's mind, and
he felt completely at peace with the world again. Dasaratha of-
fered him his blessings and a few words of guidance, and bade
farewell to him. Then he took leave of Sita and Lakshmana sep-
arately, and returned to his place in heaven.

When this was over, the gods counselled Rama, "Tomorrow,
the fifth day of the full moon, you will be completing the four-
teenth year of your exile and it is imperative that you reappear
in Ayodhya on completion of this term. Bharatha waits for you
at Nandigram single-mindedly. If you do not appear there at the
precise hour we dread to think what he may do to himself."

Rama realized the urgency and turning to Vibishana asked, "Is
there any means by which you can help me return to Ayodhya
within a day?"

Vibishana said, "I will give you the Pushpak Vimana. It was
Kubera's at one time; later Ravana appropriated it for his own
use. It will take you back to Ayodhya within any time you may
wish." He immediately summoned the Vimana to be brought.

Rama ascended this vehicle, taking with him an entire army
and all his supporters, such as Vibishana, Sugreeva, and others,
who were unwilling to part from him, and started back in the
direction of Ayodhya. As they flew along, he pointed out to
Sita various landmarks that he had crossed during his cam-
paign, and when they crossed the northern portals of Lanka he
pointed out to her the spot far below where Ravana had finally
fallen. They flew over mountains and forests; every inch of
ground had a meaning for Rama. He made a brief descent at
Kiskinda, where Sita had expressed a desire to gather a com-
pany of women to escort her when she re-entered Ayodhya. His
next halt was at the ashram of Sage Bharadwaj, who had been
hospitable to him once. At this point, Rama dispatched Hanu-
man to go forward in advance to Nandigram and inform
Bharatha of his coming.

At Nandigram, Bharatha had been counting the hours and re-
alized that the fourteenth year was nearly over. There was no

sign of Rama yet; nor any news. It seemed as though all his austerities and penances of all these years were fruitless. He looked forlorn. He had kept Rama's sandals enthroned on a pedestal and was reigning as a regent. He summoned his brother Sathrugna and said, "My time is up. I cannot imagine where Rama is gone or what fate has overtaken him. I gave my word to wait for fourteen years and in a few moments I will have passed it. I have no right to live beyond that. Now I pass on my responsibilities to you. You will go back to Ayodhya and continue to rule as a regent." He made preparations to immolate himself in fire.

Sathrugna argued and tried to dissuade Bharatha in various ways, but Bharatha was adamant. Luckily, just at this moment, Hanuman arrived in the form of a brahmin youth, and the first thing he did was to put out the fire. Bharatha asked, "Who are you? What right have you to extinguish a fire I have raised?"

Hanuman explained, "I have brought you a message from Rama. He will be here presently."

Bharatha would not believe him, whereupon Hanuman assumed for a moment his gigantic form, explaining who he was, and then narrated to Bharatha all the incidents that had taken place these fourteen years. "Now make a public announcement of Rama's coming," he concluded, "and let all the streets and buildings be decorated to receive him."

This changed the whole atmosphere. Bharatha immediately dispatched messengers to the city and made preparations to receive Rama and lead him to his rightful place back in Ayodhya.

Shortly, Rama's Vimana arrived. Rama's mothers, including Kaikeyi, had assembled at Nandigram to receive him. The reunion was a happy one. The first thing that Rama did was to discard his austere garments. He groomed and clothed himself as befitting a King, and he advised Sita to do likewise. Vasishtha received the new King and Queen and fixed the hour for the coronation, interrupted fourteen years before.

Epilogue

Rama entered Ayodhya, after fourteen years of exile, a time during which he rid this world of evil forces that had tormented it for centuries. It was a happy reunion at the capital. The coronation festivities interrupted fourteen years before were resumed. All Rama's friends and supporters were around him. Hanuman and Sugreeva and all the rest from Kiskinda were there in human form, in order to conform to the physical features of their hosts. Vibishana, Ravana's successor at Lanka, also was an honoured guest. Rama was surrounded by his mother and stepmothers, even Kaikeyi having shed her harshness by now. The kings of the earth were there and also all the gods in human form. For Bharatha it was a time of supreme satisfaction; his vow to see his brother on the throne was after all being fulfilled. The time of trials and sacrifices had ended for everyone.

At an auspicious hour of a chosen day Rama was crowned as the emperor. He sat on the throne with Sita beside him under the "white umbrella of the state" (as described by Dasaratha), holding in his right hand his Kodanda, the bow which had served him so well all these years. Lakshmana stood one step behind him, devoted and watchful, and Hanuman knelt at his feet, looking up, with his palms pressed in worship, ready to spring into action at the slightest command.

Hanuman, when he was young, as we saw in an earlier chapter, had been advised by his father to dedicate his life in the service of Vishnu. He had followed this advice without a second thought from the moment he realized that Rama was none other than the incarnation of Vishnu. Hanuman is said to be present wherever Rama's name is even whispered. At a corner of any hall, unnoticed, he would be present whenever the story of Rama is narrated to an assembly. He can never tire of hearing about Rama, his mind having no room for any other object. The traditional narrator, at the beginning of his story-telling, will always pay a tribute to the unseen Hanuman, the god who had compressed within himself so much power, wisdom, and piety. Hanuman emerges in the Ramayana as one of the most important and worshipful characters; there is a belief that to meditate on him is to acquire immeasurable inner strength and freedom from fear.

The story of Rama actually concludes with the enthronement of Rama, but in a traditional narration the story-teller would show great reluctance to reach the end. He will describe in minute detail, as Kamban has done, the arrangements for the coronation, the antecedents of the guests, and the glorious impressions that they carried in their minds when they returned home after enjoying Rama's hospitality for one full month.

During his narration the story-teller would not miss any chance for a contemporary reference. He would compare the Pushpak Vimana to a modern airliner, with the additional capacities that it could be piloted by mere thought and that its space could expand to accommodate as many as would want to get into it. One may remember that Rama invited an entire army to travel with him when leaving Lanka. On another occasion the narrator would have referred to the "Bala" and "Adi-Bala" mantras as a kind of air-conditioning in those days (p. 11). With such occasional flashes of modernity he would enliven his narration, but in the main he would know all the ten-thousand five hundred stanzas of Kamban by heart and quote them freely in song or verse, and also make his narrative significant with philosophical and religious interpretations now and then. His oral narrative would cover, in the course of forty days, the whole period from Rama's birth to his coronation, and would be addressed to an audience numbering anywhere from a couple of hundred to thousands, each instalment of narration occupying not less than three hours. On a special occasion, such as the episode of Rama's marriage, of course, he would

slow down and go into details of the wedding, and would be re-
warded by his audience with gifts of clothes and money, and
he himself would distribute sweets to celebrate the occasion.
Again, when Hanuman presented Rama's ring to Sita at Asoka
Vana, the audience, having subscribed among themselves,
would present him with a gold ring. And when he brought the
story to its pleasant conclusion, the portrait of Rama enthroned
would be carried in a procession with lights and music.

I am omitting a sequel which describes a second parting be-
tween Rama and Sita, with the latter delivering twins in a for-
est, and concluding with Rama and Sita leaving this world and
returning to their original home in the heavens. But this part of
the story is not popular, nor is it considered to be authentic, but
a latter-day addition to Valmiki's version. Kamban does not
take note of this sequel but concludes his tale on the happy note
of Rama's return to Ayodhya, followed by a long reign of
peace and happiness on this earth. And there I prefer to end my
own narration.

R. K. NARAYAN

Glossary

areca—a variety of palm
ashram—hermitage
asthra—weapon, missile or arrow powered by supernatural forces
asura—a demon
Brahma Rishi—an enlightened sage
dharba—a stiff grass generally collected for ritual purposes
durbar—court
Gandharva—a supernatural being
mantra—syllables with magic potency
margosa—a shade tree whose leaves are bitter
Maya—illusion
musth—a secretion on the forehead of an elephant during mating season
Pushya—a star
rakshasa—a demon
sadhu—a recluse or saint
sanyasi—an ascetic
shastra—scriptures
simsupa—a tree
vanji—a rare flowering creeper, which blooms once in twelve years
veena—a stringed musical instrument
yagna—a sacrifice
yaksha—a demigod
yojana—a measure of distance, usually of about 5 miles

The Guide
Introduction by Michael Gorra

Raju's first stop after his release from prison is the barbershop. Then he decides to take refuge in an abandoned temple along the banks of the river Sarayu. Raju used to be India's most corrupt tourist guide, but now a peasant mistakes him for a holy man. Gradually, almost grudgingly, he begins to play the part. He succeeds so well that God Himself intervenes to put Raju's new holiness to the test. Set in Narayan's fictional town of Malgudi, *The Guide* is the greatest of his comedies of self-deception.

ISBN 0-14-303964-4

Malgudi Days
Introduction by Jhumpa Lahiri

Introducing this collection of stories, R. K. Narayan describes how in India "the writer has only to look out of the window to pick up a character and thereby a story." *Malgudi Days*, featuring short fiction written over a period of almost forty years, is the marvelous result. Here Narayan portrays an astrologer, a snake charmer, a postman, a vendor of pies, and *chappatis*—all kinds of people, drawn in full color and endearing domestic detail. And under his magician's touch the whole imaginary city of Malgudi springs to life, revealing the essence of India and of human experience.

ISBN 0-14-303965-2

The Painter of Signs
Introduction by Monica Ali

For Raman the sign painter, life is a familiar and satisfying routine. A man of simple, rational ways, he lives with his pious aunt and finds pleasure in his creative work. But all that changes when he meets Daisy, a thrillingly independent young woman who wishes to bring birth control to the area. Hired to create signs for Daisy's clinics, Raman finds himself smitten by a love he cannot understand, much less stop—and soon realizes that life isn't so routine anymore.

ISBN 0-14-303966-0

The Ramayana
A Shortened Modern Prose Version of the Indian Epic
Introduction by Pankaj Mishra

A sweeping tale of abduction, battle, and courtship played out in a universe thronged with heroes, deities, and demons, *The Ramayana* has been thrilling readers and listeners since the fourth century B.C. Here, R. K. Narayan—one of India's greatest literary lights—draws mostly on the work of the eleventh-century Tamil poet Kamban and recounts it with the narrative flair of a master novelist. Narayan's *Ramayana* is an ancient treasure to be savored as much for its wisdom, spiritual depth, and insight as for its colorful portrayal of otherworldly passion and strife.

ISBN 0-14-303967-9